CW00567439

2nd Edition

Bessemerstraße 82, 10. OG Süd, 12103 Berlin
www.lbellpub.com
rlbell.publishing+contact@gmail.com
Cover Art: Robert Bellin

ISBN: 979-8-40909-270-2

Emotions are what drives us onward.

But are they really just signals in our heads?

PROLOGUE

THE CRIME OF CREATION

The shards of a mirror slowly rotated in place as they drifted through the black, its silver splinters reflecting a gray gallery of paintings. As they passed by, images of cities glinted up in a flash, broken in the next by sprawling forests, lush fields, or wastelands covered with graves. In short, it were a lot of contrasts displayed by the shards, and yet, they shared a single trait: The world they showed had just been destroyed. Everything was over.

Or it should have been.

Standing between the murdered memories was a group of three people. They were the cause of this disaster and looked at least somewhat upset. "I don't think this is what she meant," remarked an uncertain voice, belonging to a middle-aged man with long, disheveled hair. His sunken eyes were constantly closed, blind to the way ahead, for he was the Dealer that Gave History. It was a silly title, considering that with their old world gone, no history was left to give.

In response to his remark, the Grandmother of Gossiping Worms, his companion, nodded her wrinkled head. "You are right," she agreed with aged voice and shifted on top of her seat, a mountain of a million Worms cascading from her head. Her minions, however, usually so talkative, were silent. With everyone dead, no gossip remained they could whisper to each other.

"However, didn't they look different right after we lost?" The Grandmother's words held a trace of sadness as she remembered, and she wasn't wrong in her observation. The shards did indeed not appear the same as before. "What happened?" At her perfectly reasonable question, the last of their group started to yell.

"Why do you ask *me*, hag!? While *you* were asleep, *I* wrote the perfect story to patch up this mess, and yet, it didn't work! Clearly, *someone* must have made some kind of mistake!" The person who had spoken was a formless man, with neither hands nor head, and yet a stylish beret floating above him. Like everyone else, he was chained by his name, turned into the Poet who Omits Endings and Beginnings.

"You have done what?!" The blood of the Dealer froze in his veins, and he hurriedly took out his Diary. It was a thick book that was home to all records of the past, and it confirmed his fears. This had never been part of the plan. "Why did you simply start on your own?"

The beret floating in the air was silent as the shards of the world fell like leaves all around them. It was indeed like the Dealer had said. Right before everyone else had woken up, the Poet had tried to fulfill Her Wish, and yet, he failed, completely and utterly. There was nothing he could say in defense, so naturally, the Dealer didn't receive an answer either. "Ugh." The blind man snapped shut his Diary, massaging his temple while the Grandmother hid her face between her Worms. But unlike her and the Dealer, her Worms were extremely elated about the Poet's selfishness. With this, they had something to gossip again!

"The Poet who can't do anything!"
"True to his name!"
"Typical, isn't it?"
"I always knew he was stupid!"
"Let's call him the Dull Poet instead!"

On, and on, and on their mean mouths jeered below their hollow eyes, their bodies swaying around the Grandmother's head. As usual, the target of their taunts soon couldn't take it anymore and grabbed something from the void.

"YE NO MORE BRAIN THAN STONE, WORMS!" The Poet glared at the writhing mass from eyes that could not be seen. "YE THINK YE CAN DO BETTER?! FINE!" Enraged, the quill and inkwell he had taken out were thrown at the Worms, but before either could come close, both items disappeared without a trace. Seeing that pitiful display, the mass of slithering strings quickly formed a mocking choir, whirling around their owner as they sang:

A Poet who cannot create
can too not hope to silence us

no matter what he did or does
how verily ridiculous.

"How *dare* you!" The Poet threateningly stomped closer while the Worms just repeated their song, at least until the Grandmother finally decided to stop their insanity. "That's enough I think," she said admonishingly and hit her own head, sending a stir through the slithering ranks growing from it. "We are as responsible for this mess as he is." The Poet snorted in satisfaction when the Worms fell silent at that bitter truth. This was simply what happened if no one paid attention to him.

"Isn't this bad though?" The Dealer eventually asked the important questions. "What should we do now!?" Although his tone sounded extremely hysterical, there really was no reason to be so. It was just that, in return for his knowledge about the past, the Dealer had difficulties coping with the future.

"You idiot! What do you think!?" the Grandmother yelled. "This does not keep us from creating our new world in any way!"

"And who is supposed to do that!" Shrieking so, the Dealer turned to the Poet for some reason, but the person in question, was strangely silent, preferring to clean his fingernails although no one could see them. After all, his hands, too, were entirely transparent.

Seeing the crazy behavior of her companions, the Grandmother suddenly couldn't take it anymore. "By the Source, why are men so dull-witted?" Sometimes, it felt like she was the only one who had retained her sanity, but as if to object, the Worms on her head started to giggle maniacally. Her face twitched, but she let them be. Most of the time, it was best to ignore her minions. "Listen," she spoke to the others above their laughter. "This changes nothing. If the Poet is not able to, *I* will create our new world instead." Her confident declaration, however, met mixed feelings in the minds of her companions, for while the Dealer was simply nervous that he would have to deal with the future, the Poet had been angry the whole time. This new world was so important, and yet, he wasn't able to contribute to it at all. What if the Grandmother and her accursed vermin, spawn of all the bad rumors, would defile Her Legacy? Sick at the thought alone, he knew that he couldn't watch this, and so turned away from the other two. As he started to walk off into the darkness, the Grandmother didn't even notice him leave, but at least the Dealer still cared about him a little.

"Where are you going?" he called after him, mystified by his destination. Except for the frozen memories of the dead, there was nothing to look at, nothing left to visit. Was he trying to kill himself now that everything was over?

For a moment, the Poet stopped at the words of his old friend. "I think I will search for new inspirations." His words carried a grand tone, and yet, they rang strangely hollow through the void. "But please," the

Poet added, "do have fun smearing something onto these pages."

With a frown, the Dealer continued to watch until the Poet was finally eclipsed by the shards. Even before everything went wrong, he had always been a weird fellow, so he was sure that one day, they would meet again and have a drink. Just like the old times…

Speaking of drinks. The Dealer hurriedly faced the Grandmother. He had to make sure that there was something tasty to share with the Poet when he returned, and so he quickly joined their great work. It was a pity though. For he simply did not know yet that he and the Poet were never meant to meet again.

"So they took the Page of Beginning, the last from the Dealer's Diary, and on it, they wrote the first sentence of a new dawn:

As it ended with our feelings, so will it begin. The present, that is now the past, we leave, to step from loss and into peace. A last glimpse, and the world will be wiped clean; removed all our grief.

Heeding their words, the frozen shards of the old world burst apart, and their dust formed to weightless tears that whitened the black around them.

Rejoin what is left to an endless sea.

Drying Ink that made the weightless weighted, tears rained from the sky to form a flood gathering below. Its endless flow soon swelled up to a mighty ocean, a stormy place with waves befitting of its scale. And thus, it was called the Eternal Sea.

Inside its depths, let arrive spheres made of space.

Cascades of water along polished globes, until countless holes seemed to bob on the blue surface.

And let their darkness be filled with worlds.

Ripples spreading, like ink in water seeping life into the black, continents restored and worlds imagined.

And where another world will settle, let its globe swim in the stormy currents. On paths that ever cross, they venture forth, into the unknown time where places die and places are reborn.

With that, the water rushed left and right, right and left, dancing the worlds on its palms like snowflakes on a stormy night. And just like this, it came to be: That ending begot beginning, and beginnings beget ends."

As the Dealer put down his Pen, the Grandmother heaved a weary breath: To their feet laid creation.

"It is done," the Dealer said, completely fulfilled, and the Grandmother nodded at his side. Finally, there was history to give again, and gossips left to whisper. It made him look down at his old Diary, filled with records of their past, good and bad. What an honor that the last of its pages was carrying their new world, Her final legacy. "I have a good feeling about this. We must do everything to succeed."

The Grandmother gave a tired grin as her Worms started to bunch up at her side. "I feel the same way," she said hoarsely and reached into the mass of strings while the Dealer smiled next to her. Had he always been so naive? At her idle thought, her hand fell down, stabbing a biting blade into the Dealer's back. It cut his oh so impervious skin, the ribs and lungs and bones behind it, eventually piercing through on the other side. But it wasn't just any weapon. Groaning, the Dealer stared at the letter now protruding from his chest, not quite able to believe it. He knew well about its contents, for this was the only record of the past he considered meaningless. How... was this possible?

While the Dealer was frozen, the Diary was ripped from his hands. "I will be taking this." The Grandmother's voice purred into his ears, making him shiver. "I didn't want to do it, but you simply know too much, and, isn't it like you said? I have to do everything to succeed." With a squelch, the Grandmother's hand dislodged from the Dealer, sending him plummeting towards the Sea. Despite his imminent death, however, he only had eyes for the letter in his chest.

"Oh, Mary…" he whispered from cold lips. "Forgive me." Then, his wet grave swallowed him.

Floating alone above the ocean, the Grandmother of Gossiping Worms looked on as the Dealer vanished in the dark Sea, not even her minions interrupting. The only thing that remained of her former friend was the letter bobbing on the waves.

"Finally he's gone." It was one of her many Worms. "I never liked that antiquated dud." A few of the others nodded in agreement, while a few shook their heads. One of them, golden in color, started to circle in front of the Grandmother's head to speak. "Why did you do this?" Faced with that question, the old woman furrowed her gray brows.

"Why shouldn't I? This is for the best."

"Really?" spoke the golden one. "Then why are you crying?"

Crying? The Grandmother lifted a hand to her wrinkled face where she found the tear the golden Worm had mentioned. But she didn't feel sad. So… "Why am I crying?" The Worms around her all started to giggle at her confusion. Why did she kill her former companion, annoying as he may have been? Staring at the tiny drop of water from her eyes, she saw the lights reflected from their new world. Was there a tiny trace of color, there, deep inside its depths? As the Grandmother realized it, her hand lost all its strength, and the tear was sent spinning back into the ocean. Looking around as if she expected someone to suddenly appear, the worms laughed as she fled from the scene of her crime, fled from the worlds below that slowly set out to the future. She had found an answer to her questions. And it frightened her.

[FEATHERS' 1] DEMONS, HR, AND PAPERSNIPS

EONS LATER

What I now consider the beginning started in Caldette, a quaint town built on an endless plain bordering a sea of trees. It was an untamed thicket, only known as the Spleeping Woods, a no-man's-land so forbidding that it even divided the two largest nations of this world. Over time, many a merchant had lost their life trying to cross the shades below its canopy, and while this may seem like a waste, their stubbornness had not been in vain. For without their sacrifice, the northern trade route cutting through the woods, through the plains in the south, wouldn't exist, and Caldette, the last station before the green, would not be standing here either.

In front of the gate of that very town, two seedy city guards faced the woods in the distance. Although they were supposed to keep watch, this was the end of an extremely uneventful day, prompting the older of the guards to send his gaze over the countless cabbage fields growing around Caldette. As the proof of the work of countless farmers, they were a sight he connected many memories with, but he was suddenly pulled from the past.

"Something's coming." It was his younger colleague, shaking him from his lethargy. The old guard squinted, scrutinizing the edge of the forest in return, but the sky was now dark, and his eyes not the best anymore. Or maybe, it was just the evening mist that had risen up by now.

"Are you sure?" he asked his colleague when he couldn't spot anything. No merchant would move through the woods at night, and they rarely came this time of the year anyway. But then again, humans weren't the only visitors they had to contend with out here…

The other guard nodded in response, a short gesture, but one that invoked more than enough anxiety in the old guard. His sweaty hands reached to his left and for the spear leaning on the city wall, and now he could see the patch of black that had separated from the forest's edge, beginning to move down the road and towards them. The fog hung everywhere, hiding all its details, and the guards tensed up as it approached. Suddenly, a gust of wind picked up over the fields that were now blue with night, scattering the veil of mist and playing strangely with the clothes it uncovered: A dark coat over worn out boots. A face hidden by a broad hat. An ominous sight, carrying a bindle behind its back. Wait. A bindle?

The guards heaved a relieved breath, calming slightly as the shape arrived at the gate, and when its head turned up, a sharp face came into view. It was thin and pale, belonging to a blond man who wore a mustache and goatee that turned his face even sharper. He had a dangerous air about him, like the crazy kind you didn't want to have as an enemy, and that impression fit the playful glint in his eyes and the fact that he came from the Spleeping Woods all alone. Looking at him, the older guard wasn't sure it would be wise to let him enter the city.

"Hey there." The unknown man waved and cast a look at the darkening sky. "City's still open, right?" Before the guard could ask what he was planning to do inside, the traveler continued. "I just wanted to take a break. That forest was just horrible... You do have an inn, don't you?"

"Y-yes, two of them even," the old guard finally found his tongue, now breaking out into a smile. "However, its *so* late, I don't think they still have space for the likes of you. I might be wrong though." Although the guard's voice sounded deliberately light, it was a forced tone, one the traveler had heard so often that he had stopped to count. Almost out of habit, he took a few coins from his pockets. Was it because of his looks? Should he start to wear a bag over his head?

"And how much is the entrance fee in case you are wrong?"

When the guard heard that, a yellowed smile appeared on his face to highlight the silent understanding between them. "*Usually*, the price's three Stern per head."

"Of course it is." In response, six gray coins headed for the palm of the guard, prompting a sigh from the traveler. Even three would have been too much. Those cutthroats.

“Open up for one, please!” After biting one of the coins, the guard shouted up to the gate behind him, and the heavy beam shutting it lifted with a bang. “I would stick to the Favored Cup if I were you. The inn is straight ahead, you can't miss it.” With this, the guard turned to his younger colleague, dismissing the traveler. “Let's close up for today.”

Taking a last longing look at his coins, the traveler left the guards to their ‘work’ and passed through the small gate and onto the stage of the town beyond. A paved main street greeted him on the other side, lined with small but well off buildings. At this hour, the citizens inside were already sleeping soundly, the windows passing by as the traveler walked dark and deserted. Like silent witnesses, they watched his heels click by until the last of them fell away, the houses revealing a small market square. Right across its deserted pavement stood a clock tower rising over the rest of the city, and left and right of it two buildings not much smaller. Like siblings in an age-old standoff, they glared at each other over the square despite looking awfully similar: Both of them were large, double story buildings. Both of them were inns, and both were still illuminated. But not both were equally successful. If anything, it was frighteningly easy to recognize that the left inn had seen better days, its wooden walls gray with age and the blinds barely holding on to their window frames. Dreary and deserted were the only words to describe it.

In contrast, the inn on the right side was all the more lively, as if to make up for its broken counterpart. It was warm and bright, and even from far away, the boisterous noise inside was clearly audible. Looking at its entrance and the sign of a cup that dangled there, it was likely the inn the guard had recommended, but the traveler was not keen on following his advice. Walking on, he approached not the warm and inviting, but the odd one of the inns. Arriving at its door, the only new and sturdy thing about it, he tried to enter when he noticed something strange: It was locked.

Frowning, the traveler pushed up the brim of his hat and glanced at the windows, but the faint light inside told him that he had not been mistaken. This inn was indeed open, so he started knocking to make himself known. The first few times, no one answered his call, but he simply tried again and again. Now that he had put his mind to staying here, he would not leave until he got a reply – and his stubbornness paid off.

Another knock later, a loud noise tumbled across the floor on the other side of the door as someone stepped up to it. A wave of clicking sounds later, countless locks disengaged, an amount of security highly unusual for such a simple town. It seemed the traveler had been right. This inn was definitely the more interesting choice – and interesting was all that he had left. Holding his breath, he waited until the door opened a tiny gap, revealing the face of a tall, gaunt man whose features soured as soon as he noticed the stranger on his doorstep. “What do you want?” the innkeeper asked gruffly, his tone annoyed and uncaring of the traveler’s shady appearance.

“This is an inn, right?” he asked in return, doubtful due to the innkeeper’s harsh tone. “I’m stopping here for the night, so I was planning to get a room and some food?”

For a second, the innkeeper stared at the vagabond like he had suddenly sprouted another head. “Are you out of your mind? Did you miss the *utterly* perfect inn on the other side?” His tone carried a clear note of bitterness as he pointed past the traveler and at the inn he had just mentioned.

“No, I didn’t. But I like it better here.”

The innkeeper scoffed. No one had said that and meant it seriously for a long time. About to send the jester away, he suddenly paused. Perhaps, this kind of customer was exactly what he needed right now. “Alright, you can stay. Rooms are four Leni, meals are a half.” The traveler nodded, not doubting the cheap price, and the innkeeper opened the door to point inside. While not a single customer sat in the empty taproom beyond, nor at the counter at its far end, the wear on the floor betrayed that this place must have been well frequented at some point. The traveler nodded in approval as he saw those traces of the past. In addition to odd things, he also liked places with some history.

After the entrance was locked, the innkeeper disappeared past the counter to fetch a key and a lantern, which he handed over for his payment. “Your room is at the end of the second floor,” he explained, suddenly all smiles. “I’ll bring your food upstairs, but it might take a while.”

The traveler, tired from the journey through the forest, nodded wordlessly and moved up the stairs at the side of the room. This way, he couldn’t see the dirty smile of the innkeeper as he hurried into the backroom once more.

The innkeeper bent down, unlocking the hatch to the basement. Not in his wildest dreams would he have expected a customer today, but he knew that the time was right. He could feel it with every fiber of his being: This was an opportunity that couldn’t be wasted. With a resolute pull, the hatch screeched open, revealing the dark basement waiting below. Although he’d given his only lantern to that customer, his steps remained steady as he moved down the damp stairs and into the darkness. There, a cluttered desk came into view, barely visible beneath the books and tools scattered over its surface. Blindly and with hands nervous from excitement, the innkeeper felt around for a matchstick, holding it to a mess of candles towering right over the desk. He could still remember a time when there had been just a single one of them, how the mountain of wax had grown with each night he spent down here. Lost in thought, a small flame flared up around one of the many wicks, and the innkeeper turned around as the work of his past months appeared from within the shadows. On the floor, on the walls, a mandala of charred symbols had been smeared over every inch of the basement, its tiny, jagged symbols invoking anxiety in anyone who saw them. The innkeeper, however, remained unbothered by the uncanny sight, stepping up to the center of the circle and a spot so empty it was clear that something was still missing. A knife appeared in his hand, slightly shaking due to his nervousness. Today was the day he would finally show them who was right.

Knock, knock, we rap at the sleeping Gate.
Deliver us from desire.

As the metal bit into his hand, crimson unfolded in the center of the circle, weightlessly blooming out of the innkeeper's hand. Although he only stared for a second, by the time he looked down again, the black symbols surrounding him on all sides were already on the move. Like they were a storm and he the eye, they converged on his blood, and he was barely fast enough to jump over their rising surge before they formed a barrier around the center. Each of its layers revolved in a different direction, and while he treated his hand, he tried to get a glimpse past the dancing symbols. A second later, crimson light flashed through the gaps, its rays piercing his eyes with their brightness. With a pained shout, he shielded his eyes, but the sound of the ocean and the smell of the sea made him peek through his fingers despite the lesson he had just learned. This way, he saw that the swirling barrier around the circle was slowly receding – and now, *something* was standing inside of it.

First came its horns, two black moons over a square face, supported by a body much stronger than the strongest brute he had ever seen. The ash purple scales covering most of its skin were stretched tight over its bulging muscles, covered sparsely by obsidian armor, and the sight of the black shards sticking to it here and there were just as savage as the tail unwinding in the background or the sharp claws growing from its fingers. But the most jarring part about this monster were its legs. Compared to that of a human, they had one segment too many and ended in huge feet, with nails that scratched deep furrows into the floor. Seeing how the monster stood, like a feral animal prowling on its toes, even the most stupid person would realize that they were before a predator. But this wasn't just a simple monster, it was a *demon:* Cunning and evil.

While the innkeeper stared in fright, the demon unfroze, finally touching his feet onto the ground. Once more, the fresh air of a new world streamed through his nostrils before his eyes opened, revealing two coals glowing inside his skull. When he saw where he had been called to, the demon's mouth opened, and an amused chuckle spilled past his rows of sharp teeth and into the room. It was a distorted tune, produced by an otherworldly voice deeper than the darkest of nights.

Oh ye who plea and stir the Gates of the Den, its Hand has arrived in answer. State your business.

Dazed by the thundering words that resounded in his bones, the innkeeper remained frozen until the demon's burning glare suddenly made him hurry to answer. He knew how this went! He had read about it before!

"R-right. There is an inn on the o-o-other side of the c-city. A-and–"

Stop your stuttering! Who is supposed to understand you this way!?

Annoyance rolled off the demon, and the innkeeper stumbled back. His eyes glanced over the last black runes wrapped around the monster, trying to reassure himself. As long as he didn't step past them, he would be safe. Everything was fine. Taking a deep breath, he continued. "The inn on the other side of this city. I want it gone."

...That's everything?

The demon almost sounded doubtful, his expectations of a difficult mission betrayed. Still, if this task really was as easy as it appeared, he would simply take it as an added bonus before he went on Break Day. The innkeeper, however, seemed angry at his question.

"What do you mean, 'everything?!' They *ruined* me and didn't even try to let me save face, rubbing it

under my nose every single day! They *have* to pay."
At that, the demon nodded slowly, happy about the grudge the human was displaying, and opened his arms in a welcoming gesture. The barrier around him turned milky where his claws approached.

Then I will deal with that inn for you. But what, I wonder, do you plan to offer in return?

Relieved that the first step had been taken, the innkeeper stepped closer, a grin spreading across his gaunt face. The books had said that there was only one thing demons wanted, souls, and luckily, he had happened across a little gift today. "I have a customer upstairs, a traveler. No one will miss him, so do with him what you want."

Hearing that, the demon broke out in a grin just like the innkeeper, although his was a little more toothy. For a moment, he closed his eyes and sniffed the air before glancing back down through half closed lids.

Yes. A good offering indeed.

That was exactly what the innkeeper had wanted to hear. But then, as if to top it off, the demon thoughtfully put a hand to his square chin and continued.

But it's *too* good for so little work. How about I give you a discount the next time you request the services of the Den? What do you say?

Of course, the innkeeper's mood only improved by leaps and bounds at that courteous offer. Not only could he avoid offering up his own soul because of that traveler, he even got a discount! He was so grateful to that wretch, he almost considered digging a proper grave for him once everything was over. "Yes! Yes, thank you, that sounds great!"

Still smiling, the demon clapped: Everything according to protocol. Suddenly, a large scroll appeared in the air and dropped to the floor, unrolling all the way to the innkeeper's feet. The entire length of the line of parchment was covered in tiny writing, so small that it was difficult to read, and the innkeeper gulped as he faced the wall of text.

Don't worry. This is a *completely* standard contract. You don't need to read it.

For a moment, the innkeeper was tempted to agree, but then, he remembered that the books had warned about trusting demons. They were deceitful by nature, always trying to take as much as you let them, and only the words in their contract, such as the scroll at his feet, kept them from betraying their summoners. This was the reason it was so important to pay attention to them, and while the innkeeper may have been a bitter, angry man, he wasn't stupid. "Let me take a look at it anyway," he told the demon in a firm voice, although his legs were shaking. A distorted sigh later, the rest of the scroll was shoved over the barrier. The demon didn't resent the innkeeper for his cautiousness, but watching him read the endless contract was incredibly boring, mostly because his summoner was obviously inexperienced. Although the runes of the text instantly entered the minds of their readers, understood by anyone and anything, his gaze following the text like a snail, struggling with even the simplest of the complicated implications. To the innkeeper, it clearly was an exhausting task that took plenty of time, so when the sea of words had finally run dry, his head still felt like it was swimming.

"A-Alright," he confirmed, his voice hoarse. "Add that you are not allowed to wreck my inn, and I agree." The demon's eyes flared up when he heard that, and he clapped his hands together in relief. A glowing quill appeared in response, pointed to a blank line in the contract. There was only one thing left keeping him from his meal, from the end of this mission, and from his long-awaited Break Day.

Sign the contract, and all you wish for will come true.

So the innkeeper gripped the quill tightly and wrote down his name.

With the arrival of the night, the homes of Caldette turned into dark silhouettes, their roofs like the peak of a mountain range below the starry sky. The only thing that broke the jagged line of their roofs was the clock tower in the center of the city, its pointed tip cutting into the biggest of the three moons like a knife. Framed by the circle of blue light, a sinister shape could be seen standing, smoldering red eyes trained on a building below. It was the inn his summoner had mentioned, and as the demon studied the bright and cheery hubbub taking place inside, the last of his doubts that this was more than a small-town squabble fell away. Had he really been called just for this?

With a shrug, he jumped off the roof and down to the light-filled inn, landing with a grace on top of its small chimney that belied his size. Steam and smoke billowed out from below and up to his sensitive nose, and the smell he caught made him pause for a moment. It was the smell of the handiwork of his people.

Surprised to find the signs of another demon in this little town, the demon made double sure that no dangers awaited him here. But except for the familiar smell, this building was just an ordinary inn. Along with the fact that no warning had been put out for this world, it couldn't be the scheme of some high-ranking demon either. Knowing this, he figured there was no reason to be careful. As far as his peers were concerned, he was confident he could get away with angering anyone.

Stepping down from the chimney and onto the roof, he pushed the matter to the back of his mind and lifted his arms, where a flash of crimson symbols raced from his claws and up into the night. This job was as good as done already…

The taproom of the inn 'To the Favored Cup' was jam-packed. Waitresses circled around the tables filled with customers, constantly ready to take up orders, to serve meals, and to hand out drinks. Farmers, merchants, and their wives cheerily sat together, disregarding the usual social boundaries of rank and status. It was quite an unusual sight, especially for a wealthy human village like Caldette.

At the far end of the brimming room stood a counter, and the portly, middle-aged woman behind it was currently preparing another round for her customers. A broad smile graced her lips as she took one bottle after another from the shelf behind her, humming a merry tune. Autumn was always a good time for her and her business. With the harvest season over and the winter crops out on the field, there was little to do for the farmers but to find their way into her establishment. And before the harsh winter came and froze over their pockets, there was always enough money for her to steal with her services.

Putting down the bottle she was holding, the woman looked upon her regulars. There was something to this night, a special quality that made her feel nostalgic. Things hadn't always been this rosy. When she just opened up, she had been young and hopeful and full of dreams, thinking that she would make it easily if she could just scrape together enough money to set up shop. But competing with the inn on the other side had been harder than she thought, and her dreams quickly soured into envy. That was when she realized that she had to do something, anything to search for a way to change that.

A grin sneaked onto her lips at that thought. Nowadays, there was nothing a few secret ingredients couldn't fix. She still remembered the expression of the old fool across the marketplace when more and more customers decided to visit her bar instead of his filthy shack. After he had so thoroughly tried to make life hard for her, she had been eager to return the favor in kind and do everything to bring him down, and with success! It didn't take long until no one wanted to set foot over his doorstep again, not in small part due to the rumors she had spread. Her smile got even broader. Somehow, remembering that part of the past always managed to improve her mood.

The woman was just about to continue her work when she heard a loud noise from above. Looking up to the ceiling with a frown, everything around her turned crimson. She came to a moment after, an eternity later, sprawled on the ground in the center of a bloody mess of wooden splinters. The cheery atmosphere that had enveloped her just seconds ago had been mercilessly ripped away, and when she opened her eyes, she saw the dead bodies of her customers strewn about, the clear night's sky stretching out above her. The ceiling of her inn was completely gone, together with her guest rooms, the guests themselves, and, most importantly, her private room. *And all her money.* When she realized that, she giggled until her back hurt from the wood burrowing into it, but for some reason, she couldn't even try to pull them out. Her limbs refused to budge a single inch.

Completely helpless, she lay there like a broken doll and stared up at the sky until it filled her whole view, even louder than the agitated calls in the distance. To her, in her final moments, there was only the clear and silent night, and the sound of the crackling flames feasting on the remnants of her life's work. While the autumn wind was chilly, the fires warmed her, and then, she realized everything was gone. A single tear escaped her eye. Had she not done everything imaginable, within and beyond the boundaries of morality and immorality? She had just wanted to be successful, but now, nothing was left.

Suddenly, a sarcastic clap reached her ears, shattering the sanctity of her death. A demon came into sight, his jagged grin and gray-violet scales stirring up old memories. The monster stopped right in front of her, towering over her head and looking down at her with eyes squinted in delight.

Oh hello, little bird! Your despair is truly wonderful, but–? Could it be that you are hurt? How clumsy you are!

As the droning voice of the demon continued to mock her, it was so similar to the one in her memories, but not quite. She tried to answer, to plead for her life a final time, but she couldn't. Her mouth wouldn't move no matter how hard she tried.

Why are you so afraid?

The demon held a dented kettle into her field of view. It was the remains of the stew they had served today, as always seasoned with her special ingredient.

I can tell that this is not the first time you have seen one of us.

Of course it wasn't! How else could she have beaten that filthy innkeeper on the other side of the square!? But back then, she hadn't been lying on the floor without control of her body! She struggled to express her thoughts, to scream and shout at the damned demon who had ruined her life, but it was in vain. The kettle hurtled into a burning corner before he lifted her by the throat and closer to his stinking grin. Couldn't anyone… save her?

No. This is a fitting end for a sinner like you who doesn't know when to make up. But don't worry. I'm sure that whoever you made a contract with will have plenty of fun with your soul.

She trembled weakly in the demon's hand as she realized he was right, throwing her into deepest despair. There always was a price for dealing with demons. How could she have forgotten?

As the scaly hand of the demon clenched tight, a crunching sound rang through the night, the woman unable to understand what had happened. Just like that, her head separated from her shoulders, the last thing saw the demon holding her headless torso and the stars happily twinkling in the background. And the last thing she heard before everything went black was a voice.

This is the end. May the Purpose bring you peace.

Dropping the empty shell of a woman he was holding, the demon looked on as her soul left her body and floated up into the sky. The translucent being resembled a mix of jellyfish and octopus, the red color of its cute, round head fading as it swam to the origin of its contract, towards the Den. Looking down, the demon saw the other souls still on the ground, latched onto the heads of the customers of this inn. For such an easy mission, it was an unexpectedly fruitful harvest, all because of the poison the dead innkeeper had handed to the people here. Their souls had been so tormented by her that they now shone a clear red, and he silently thanked the unknown demon who had set up this little gift. Hurrying from corpse to corpse, he collected the cute, little lights before they could fade, and while most of them vanished with a squeak as he pressed them into his chest, stored for a later date, a few went straight to his mouth. While it was stupid to eat them without being hungry, the taste was just too heavenly to resist.

Licking his lips as he collected the last soul, the demon finished his work and looked around the devastation he had wrought. By now, most of the inn was burning, and two of its walls were on the verge of collapse. Its customers, killed by the explosion, were strewn about, but their bodies now appeared dull and soulless to his eyes. Satisfied, he grinned at the sight, deciding to leave before the rest of this ruin came down on his head, and a snapping sound spread through the night as his bat-like wings appeared to spread wide over the flames. Sparks sprayed as he flapped them once, shooting into the air just as the first people arrived to put out the fires. The gasps trailing after him were like music to his ears, and he laughed at the sign of a job well done, looking forward to his break once he returned. But before that, he still had to take care of his reward; and so, he quickly left to claim it.

UNLIKELY COMPANY

In a dusty room lit by moonslight, the traveler was laying on top of a creaky bed, his eyes half closed as he glanced at a piece of paper resting in his hands. Since he'd found it, it had been crumpled many times, and yet, it still looked like new, truly a special page with few words.

let's drink, come find me. -D

Once more, the paper was crumpled in the traveler's hand, tossed into a corner where it unfolded and disappeared before it hit the ground. One day, he had awoken with the note next to his knees, mockingly casual after the chaos that had taken place just before. And now, it had led him to this world, his goal to get answers from who had written it, to create the most exiting play in– He froze and shook his head before leaning back into his pillow. Nothing about that today, he only wanted to relax. But just as he closed his eyes, a fist knocked against the shabby door to his room.

With a groan, the traveler stood up from his creaking bed, stretching as he walked over to answer. Out in the hallway was the innkeeper, holding a wooden tray with a large bowl and an earthen mug. Its contents, thick stew and light brown ale, surprisingly promised something worth the long wait. At first, he wanted nothing more but to rip the food out of the innkeeper's hands, but then, the traveler noticed that he seemed quite nervous. The whole tray was shaking. "Is everything alright?"

"Y-yes, it's just been a while since I had a customer, that's all!" Although the traveler directed a doubtful look at the innkeeper, he didn't press the point. After all, he didn't *really* care about this minor character, it was just how he was expected to behave.

"Alright then, have a good rest." The door shutting in the innkeeper's face abruptly ended their conversation and left the traveler free to carry the tray over to the small table on the other side of the room. Because this was the second floor, the view from the window behind it was far and unobstructed, going all across the marketplace, the city, and up to the forest in the distance. Its tree greens mixed beautifully with the red roofs below the night, soothed by the light of the tranquil moons above. Lowering his gaze from the city, the traveler took a sip from his ale and sighed when it was even better than expected. He had been parched, as if the last time he drank something had been an eternity ago, and maybe it really was. It was hard to remember nowadays. But, thirst stilled, his growling stomach was next to act up, prompting an eager look at his meal and the spoon next to it. Carefully, he scooped up some stew and–

A loud explosion roared through the night, sending a flash of red blazing across the marketplace. The shock wave was so strong that it formed ripples in his stew on the table, but the only thing the traveler could see outside was the peaceful sight of the sleeping city. Even so, he regretfully halted the spoon that was teasing his tongue and heaved an annoyed sigh. This was not how he had imagined his stay! In silence, he kept holding the spoon, waiting, one, two seconds, to see if something else would happen, but no. Nothing. The spoon disappeared in his mouth: He had decided. What happened onstage while he wasn't there was none of his business. He had come here to relax – and relax he would. The rest of his meal passed uneventfully. There were no explosions. Neither cats nor dogs nor Torgs raining from the sky. Only silence.

By the time he finished his food, the first anxious calls of the villagers became audible outside, and a little tension drained from the traveler's shoulders. Hopefully, the townsfolk would take care of their own problems, but just as he lifted the mug with his ale and was about to take another sip, the door behind him opened so violently it nearly flew off its hinges. Still, it was questionable why it had been opened in the first place, because one moment later, the whole frame was ripped out of the wall completely.

Ooops.

The traveler turned around in his seat and was surprised by what he saw. Bent over the pitiful door on the ground was a being he easily recognized as a demon, and in the gap behind it stood the innkeeper, staring at that very demon in dismay.

"W-what are you doing! My door, what have you done to my door!?" His shrieks were so distraught, they were quite unlike the gruff expression he made earlier. The demon turned around holding his ears, not at all apologetic.

I tried, okay? It's an accident, not a violation of the contract. Not my fault the doors here are so flimsy.

The innkeeper's mouth gaped open silently as the demon simply turned back around to his business. With his reward and his break finally in sight, he lifted a clawed hand, crimson runes racing like lightning down to his fingers. It was a sufficiently flashy spell, and as soon as it was completed, the hapless fool sitting in the chair in front of him would come to enjoy a new existence as a pile of ash.

No offense, okay? But do me a favor and die.

Hearing that, the traveler postponed any comments about the unexpected entry and instantly tried to save the rest of his increasingly deformed evening. His mind turned at top speed, considering every possible action he could take to ensure the safety of his ale. Then, and it surprised himself, he managed to recall something from his mangled memories, something he had received long ago.

"H-ha-halt! First, what do you think about this?!" The traveler stretched out his arm, now in his hand a small leaden sphere. It was covered in runes that spoke directly to the mind, and as soon as the demon saw their jagged shapes, the spell he prepared frizzled out like a weak firecracker.

W-what?! A bulla from the Crimson Queen?! Are you kidding me!?

Losing all strength, the demon's strong arm flopped weakly to his side, his reward forgotten as he stared at the piece of metal in dismay. His mouth opened and closed while he tried to deny what his eyes were seeing, but he certainly wasn't dreaming. A shiver ran down his spine as he realized that he had been about to do something very dangerous. Why hadn't he sensed the bulla, that metal ball, sooner? If he had known about it, he would have never accepted this traveler as a reward for his contract! Now all his plans were ruined!

Seeing the demon trapped in a severe life crisis and the innkeeper lamenting his door, the traveler grinned to himself in satisfaction. While he couldn't quite remember why exactly that 'bulla' kept demons away from him, this way, his ale was saved and with it his evening. Just to be safe, though, he quickly chugged down the rest of it, still a little afraid that this particular demon would suddenly change his mind about attacking him. Unfortunately, it was that very move that provoked the demon. Seeing the traveler take a casual drink looked like blatant mockery, and his clawed hands became deadly weapons as he tensed them in anger. The rage almost scorched the inside of his chest. Maybe he could at least get away with teaching that bastard a little lesson?

Just when the situation was about to turn for the worse, a loud, angry knock crashed against the entrance to the inn below. The innkeeper flinched at the sound, looking from the broken door at his feet and towards the stairs down the taproom. Quite the commotion seemed to have gathered outside. Maybe it was the villagers, here to ask for his help? He could already imagine their pleading faces, begging for his aid, so he quickly skipped away to welcome them. The traveler didn't even notice how he left. With his meal and ale defeated, there was nothing more important to him but to sleep in a proper bed, but there was one *tiny* problem: A huge demon was standing smack dab in the center of his room – and it really didn't fit the ambiance. Now that he looked at him more closely, said demon seemed visibly shaken by the noise downstairs. His blood had drained from his face, leaving it more gray than the usual violet. It seemed something had begun to dawn on him.

Oh no... I led the villagers here... but I can't leave without... soul...

He was so perturbed that he mumbled out loud, and of course, the traveler didn't miss that chance and nudged his elbow into the demon's firm side. "What's the matter, big boy? A Leni for your thoughts?" The demon flinched, freezing for an instant before suddenly shaking off the source of all his trouble. He now understood that he wasn't about to go on break as planned, and what did he get instead? A bastard so annoying he already couldn't bear him anymore.

Stop being obnoxious! This is all your fault, so how about you try to not make it even worse! Don't you understand how important it is to wear a bulla so that everyone can see it?! Do you have any idea what you did to me?!

As the demon aired his frustrations in a bitter tone, the traveler shied away from the wave of very demonic spittle that went flying at him. When he dared to look again, the demon had fallen silent, panting and with a vein throbbing on his forehead, so he decided to try and lift his mood. Slowly, he reached up to the gigantic shoulder of his pitiful friend and gingerly patted it. "Shhh, don't worry," he said consolingly, "I know you will make it through this."

That was it! The demon was about to grab the traveler, but before he could, a mob of people stormed into the room and interrupted the strange situation between them. "THERE THEY ARE! THE DEMON AND HIS SUMMONER! GET THEM!" It was the innkeeper, standing behind a mob of angry villagers, and demon and traveler turned their heads at the same time to stare at them. The former quickly put a hand to his head, feeling a headache coming on. Today really wasn't his day. As long as his contract wasn't completed, he wasn't allowed to harm his client, and he couldn't damage this inn either because of that stupid condition. How was he supposed to get out of here now? Such a thing had never happened before.

“Whoa, you people, what are you doing in my room!?” Completely deaf to the mood, the traveler started to yell at the closest villager. The only answer he got, however, was a stab from a pitchfork which he quickly evaded. The rest of the mob didn’t seem too friendly either, lifting their farming tools higher as they started to corner the two of them. This clearly wasn’t good, the traveler thought, just about to handle this situation when a giant arm nudged into his side. By the time he finally regained his balance and looked up, he saw a grinning demon looking down at him.

You better get out through the window if you want to leave this place in one piece.

Although it may have been an unexpected solution, the demon didn't care how, he just wanted to escape this room – even if that meant relying on the help of this newfound scourge. The traveler, however, just stared at him with dull eyes, showing no intention to move. What would become of his well-deserved rest if he left? He had already paid!

DO IT!!!

“Okay, okay! No reason to get angry!” Hastily grabbing his bindle from his bed, the traveler lunged at the window behind the table, deftly kicking out the expensive glass pane along with the rest of it. His surprisingly quick escape made the demon freeze up in surprise, at least until a pitchfork scratched over the chunks of his armor. Now was not the time to think.

Imitating the traveler, he charged towards the now broken window, crashing through the hole and out into the open. While some would say that he deliberately destroyed the wall in the process, he had merely tried to jump out of a hole in the wall – the rest was just an accident.

"Nooooo! Not my window! My wall!" The demon laughed as he fell, down into pavement of the marketplace below.

A few moment earlier, when the innkeeper had heard the loud knock, he had gleefully rushed towards the door, ready to rub his superiority into the faces of the despairing villagers outside. But when he opened up, what was on the other side was not what he had expected. Rather than frightened villagers, an angry mob stood in front of his inn, complete with pitchforks and everything. It was a frightening sight that instantly sent cold shivers down his back. Did they find out already?

"Y-yes? What can I do for you?" he asked into the crowd, and a well-aged but sturdy man with a thick beard stepped forward to answer him.

"O'Leary, what is the meaning of this!? People came to me saying a demon entered your inn! What have you done!? I know things have been looking bad for you lately, but how dare you violate this final taboo!?" As the aged man ranted, the moonslight descending from the sky caught a crest engraved on his armor. It showed six arrows radiating out from a circle, their tips forming the outline of a shield with just as many sides. It was known as the Warding Shield, the crest of The Vanguard of World's Edge, and while this old Vanguard was long retired, his mind was clearly left bound by the Edge's teachings: No mercy to demons and anything coming from beyond.

The innkeeper's mind, faced with the accusations coming from the retired veteran, simply shut down. Somehow, they knew about the demon, but he couldn't plainly admit that *he* was the one who had called him. While no one knew what really happened to the summoners the Edge caught, the innkeeper had heard rumors, and none of them were good. Thus, he did the first thing that crossed his mind: Deny everything. "W-what are you talking about? A demon?! Why do you think I would ever deal with those t-terrible things?" Although his voice sounded innocent, he barely managed to prevent it from cracking, a fact that the former Vanguard in front of him didn't miss.

"Don't play games with me, O'Leary! That *abomination* entered your inn, and the fact that you are still alive is the only proof I need that you summoned it! I'm only wanted to make sure for old times' sake."

The innkeeper's brow twitched when he heard that. This was not going well. But what could he– "I know! It has to be the guest that arrived today! Y-you know me, I would never taint our beautiful town like this!" In any other circumstances, it might have been a reasonable excuse. But the reaction he got was not as expected.

"Hahaha, stop already! Who would be so stupid to visit *your* inn of all places!"

The innkeeper nervously glanced at the other villagers to gauge their reaction, but everyone seemed to agree. And if he was honest, he couldn't even resent them for it anymore. The whole town knew that he had had no customers for months. But still, there was a way to convince them. "It's really true! Come, I will take you to his room. If we actually have a demon in our town, that filthy vagabond must have brought it here!" With that, the innkeeper quickly turned around, but to the villagers, it looked more like he wanted to flee from the mob than anything else. They all shared a doubtful look before following after him.

And so, it came to be that a small stampede accompanied the innkeeper up the stairs where they had to squeeze into the narrow hallway. At its far end, a huge hole was gaping instead of a door, and a bizarre sight presented itself: A man wearing a dark cloak stood idly at the side of something that simply screamed demon. One of his arms was currently extended, patting the shoulder of the monster like someone would a pet for a job well done. The villagers all gasped in unison, and the Vanguard in their midst almost popped a vein at the sight that defied everything he had fought for all his life.

"THERE THEY ARE! THE DEMON AND HIS SUMMONER! GET THEM!" the innkeeper screamed like his life depended on it. The only way left to save his own skin was to dump all the blame onto his customer, and it seemed to work surprisingly well. After what the villagers had seen, even if that fool was caught, no one would believe him anymore. And indeed, a second later, the angry mob of villagers stormed forward and towards the room, the innkeeper all but forgotten.

Shortly after he had sprung out of the window, the demon crashed down onto the pavement and made stones burst up in all directions. Not the least bit fazed by the fall, he quickly stood up and looked around. There, in a side street, he could barely spot the traveler's coat just as it was about to disappear. Apparently, its wearer was trying to escape without a word, but he wouldn't let his reward and the man who had ruined his plans get away this easily.

HEY! WAIT!

At his loud shout, the traveler's face reappeared from behind the corner, and when he saw the demon in front of the dilapidated inn, he opted for a happy wave. "Catch me if you can!" he said playfully, then ran away even faster than before. The demon stared after him for a moment, slightly dazed by this unusual reaction. Was this what one would expect from a sane individual? What was wrong with this person? But before he could find an answer to that question, the villagers burst out of the door behind him and onto the marketplace. Their pitchforks were already trained at him, and how nice, now they had torches too. The demon quickly started to run. There was no time for this – he had to chase someone!

Leaving the villagers to eat dust, he sprinted after the traveler, chasing so fast after the edge of his coat that everything else melted to a blur. So often did it seem within reach, teasing and taunting him, but it never was, almost as if it deliberately led him through the streets. But that couldn't be, right?

Always a few steps ahead of the demon, the traveler finally decided to end their chase and moved their tracks back towards the main street. It was lined with buildings and led straight south, leading out of the city, but now that it was night, the gate at its end was tightly shut. The traveler didn't bother to open it and dashed up the stairs where he kicked open the door to the wall. The lookout on the other side almost died of shock, turning around right as the traveler plunged down the wall. For a moment, their eyes met, then separated as he sailed off into the night. The confused guard scratched his head. Was he drunk, or did someone just jump off the wall and tip his hat at him?

Meanwhile, the demon, too, had reached the main street, just in time to see the traveler disappear up the gate. He stopped in his step, confused how the distance between them hadn't shrunk but not ending his chase. Now that his prey was out of the narrow streets of the city, with no roofs to hide him, he was sure that he would win this race. A sharp snapping sound later, his wings had returned to his back, a single beat carrying him up into the starry sky. Their soundless flaps led him south and along the highway until the city fell out of sight, and there, he spied the traveler running through the darkness. With a grin, the demon dove downwards, his eyes drawing red trails through the night. Yes. There wasn't a chance that he would lose him now.

The faint light of the three moons hit a broad hat and became a shadow that shrouded the face of the traveler. His eyes flashed up from beneath as he observed the darkness around him, but he could spot neither villagers nor demons. No one was following him. For now.

Although the traveler wasn't tired, a sigh escaped his lips as he slowed his steps. He had been looking forward to a quiet night, to sleeping in a proper bed after being on the road all this time, and it would have worked out just fine if not for all the people that had suddenly decided to flock around him. At least playing with that demon had been fun, but it also left a bitter aftertaste. Now, he wouldn't get to learn what would happen to him in the future…

Just as he thought so, a high, whistling noise cut across the silent cabbage fields and crashed down right in front of his feet. Earth and greens went flying through the air, and when his bindle lowered from in front of his face, a demon-sized crater was gaping up where the road had been. And in it, what a surprise, was a demon-sized demon. The traveler had to admire his persistence, but when he saw how the demon straightened up to his full, imposing size, spread his wings wide, and trained his burning eyes down at him, he suddenly remembered why he disliked most of his kind: Demons always were such posers.

Hello there. Thought I would simply let you escape?

Totally unimpressed by the demon's flashy entrance, the traveler dusted a cabbage off his coat before replying. "My dear demon, who said I was trying to escape? I was giving you a lesson in tailing people! Now listen, here is your assessment: On a range from incompetent to quite stupid, you scored a solid seven. Isn't that nice? The lesson is over. Please leave now."

That scale doesn't even make sense! Wait, I don't even care! How dare you just up and escape without taking responsibility!? Just because you have that bulla, it doesn't change anything about the fact that I need your soul to return to the Den! Don't you understand?! I'm *trapped* in this shitty world! And it's your fault!

While the traveler *did* see his point, there was only one type of person he ever traveled with, and did he really want to return to the old ways? He thought for a second before he opened his mouth. Maybe there was a reason why coincidence had allotted him this pitiful demon. "It seems my words were a bit too complex for you, so let me rephrase: Now that your lesson is over, you *must* stop following me! A whole town thinks I'm a demon summoner because of you, and when they send the Edge after me, the last thing I need is a uselessly big demon on my tailcoat!"

U-useless?! Maybe you are the one too stupid to understand: The earlier you die, the earlier I can return, even if that means to press those angel suckers right into your face! So go, and get killed!

For a moment, the traveler pretended to be left speechless, although some of his surprise was indeed real. What an unreasonable demon this was. "Fine then," he replied eventually, the demon glaring down at him with arms crossed. "This means you are my disciple now. So come along, disciple! Come along to the end of the world – and fail miserably!" Leaving those grand and somehow patronizing words, the traveler spun past the crater in a dance to proceed along the street. As he had predicted, the demon was neither impressed nor intimidated, only more annoyed.

Disciple?! You really can't stop spouting shit, huh?! Where are you even going!? Hey! I'm talking to you here!

But the traveler didn't bother to reply, leaving the demon no choice but to follow him down the starlit street. All the while, the big lug kept up his questioning and nagging until he felt his ears start to bleed, but the traveler didn't mind, his smile flashing up as if to eclipse the unequal pair. Soon, he knew, this noisy demon would get the bill for all his suffering…

BREAKING POINT

Under the morning sky, an aged man wearing old plate armor stood in front of a ruined building. At his feet lay the charred remains of walls and tables, people and chairs. The inn that had occupied this place had burned down, leaving only a pile of dust and ash. Even the bodies had fallen apart, so they couldn't tell yet how many people were killed, but as the old Vanguard stared at the ruin, he knew that it had to be too many. Those accursed demons. He clenched his hands. Those damned summoners.

Suddenly, a quiet laughter swept over the marketplace, pulling the retired veteran away from the remains of the destroyed inn. What he saw across the pavement was another inn, ruined in a very different sense of the word until just recently. O'Leary, now the only remaining innkeeper in Caldette, was standing outside, distributing water and bread. It seemed like from now on, things wouldn't look too bleak for him anymore. The villagers he served, on the other hand, were a picture of misery. Their faces were grief-stricken and exhausted, for despite the recent casualties, they had spent the whole night fighting fires and searching for the demon. But after that abomination left them in the dust last night, it had vanished without a trace, although the same wasn't true for its summoner. If the guard at the south gate was to be believed, that scum had continued down the trade route, but no one had wanted to chase after him in the night. The Vanguard sighed in frustration, knowing that he was too old to chase after a demon summoner, but fortunately, there were others who could do so in his place. With a last look at O'Leary, he left the marketplace, his nails biting deeply into his palms as he formed the first words of a letter in his mind. All those who broke the Edge, the veil of the world, had to be punished – and like every one of its Vanguards, he would make sure of that.

About a day southwest of Caldette and the old Vanguard, the two suns in the blue sky burned down on an unending plain. The small town and the trade route leading to it had long fallen out of sight, and there was just dry, hard grass all around. Rustled by the winds, its stalks danced through the air before touching down on a broad-brimmed hat. It was the traveler, walking at the front of a trampled lane of grass, and, following at his heels, the demon. They had crossed the plains for the whole night, enduring the constant gusts that tugged at hat, coat, and tail, and although the grass whirling through the air may have looked beautiful, its bits and pieces constantly entered their mouths. The demon had complained since the first stalk, only stopping when the suns rose over the horizon, and judging from the way his shoulders were drooping, this wasn't what he had imagined when he decided to follow the traveler. It was a pitiful sight, but to understand the reason the demon had been reduced to this much, it was important to know about his home. Far away from here, the demons lived their lives in a world the truest form of a barren wasteland. It surface was so desolate that it carried no name, suffocating everything in a maelstrom of soot that slowly burned up the air. But deep below, in the very core of that husk, laid a secret, a mess of tangled tunnels worse than any labyrinth. They were so extensive no one had ever managed to reach their end, and since the exodus from Leysahrah, those very tunnels were the source of all respectable demons, the Den of Sins. Compared to the dark, sweltering depths of its halls, the sunny grassland the demon was in now should have felt like vacation – if there hadn't been so much light.

Ughhh, why is it so bright here?

"So that you are tortured better."

...

How long do we have to keep walking?

"You don't need to know."

Where are we going?

At that, the traveler spat out another load of grass before stopping in his tracks to look at the demon. It seemed the few hours of brightness didn't suffice yet to stop him from complaining for good. He had to stop him before things turned even worse. "You can be terribly annoying, do you know that?" The demon, still hunched, lifted his head, shielding his eyes against the light.

What a nice compliment. If you want me to stop, you can kill yourself at any time.

The traveler snorted at that silly joke, but the demon was quite serious. Although he was sure that this human would soon die in an unexpected accident, until then, being annoying was the only way he could take revenge for his postponed Break Day. He had had already saved souls, had made plans for it! Important plans! Just when the demon thought that, a rumble passed beneath his feet.

Did you feel that?

"What do you–" Suddenly, the earth shattered, and without warning, the head of a gigantic worm shot out of the grassy plain. It was about as thick as the demon was tall and covered all over in a dark carapace that swallowed the light of the suns. While the traveler had merely been thrown backwards by the worm's appearance, the demon now balanced on top of its head, the ground below retreating by the second. A slimy sound prompted him to look at his feet, and he jumped off the monster's large head just in time to see its maw snap open like the bud of a teeth-filled flower. With a nervous laugh, he summoned his wings to escape, but the worm simply rose higher, chasing after him with a screech. It didn't seem like it would relent anytime soon.

Down below, the traveler rolled through the grassland like a strange tumbleweed, spouting curses until he finally slowed to a stop. Covered in dirt, he jumped to his feet before glaring at the worm still chasing the demon in the air. "Where did this thing come from?!" he shouted. "I hate worms!" The demon, too, glared down at him in response, quickly changing the course he was flying on.

Really?! How about you deal with it, then?!

Now headed straight towards the traveler, the demon lead around the worm chasing after his back. This was his chance to get the reward he needed to go home! "No! My disciple, you wouldn't do this to me, would you?" Although the traveler desperately tried to evade, the demon only had to adjust his course.

Do what? Am I not even allowed to escape from a monster?

With no way to deny that, the traveler spent the rest of the time until the worm arrived running around like a headless rabbit. The demon escaped upwards just before the monster dug back into the earth, leaving a cloud of dust in its wake. Hovering in the air, he looked around, trying to make out the traveler. Did he succeed?

"What a haphazard attempt on my life!" a voice suddenly sounded from the cloud of dust which cut apart like the curtains of a stage. Behind them, the traveler appeared, extending upward from his hand a tarnished sword as huge as the demon. It's design was reminiscent of a ruffled feather, a quill with a nib on its lower end, and so it had been named the Fountain Blade. More lifelike than life, the traveler lowered the fragile looking blade at the demon in front of him, maybe in an attempt to appear threatening. But the target of his ire, seeing the ridiculously large blade, didn't even try to hold back his laughter.

What do you plan to do with that thing? Write a poem?

The traveler's eye twitched, but before he could reply, the worm reappeared from the earth – directly below the laughing demon. Surprised, he quickly tried to fly away another time but couldn't evade the ball of drool that suddenly shot up from the monster's maw. The fluid stuck to his skin like gum, invading the almost invisible joints of his wings until they screeched to a halt. The traveler laughed as the demon started to plummet towards the ground, threatening to disappear in the waiting mouth of the worm. "Disciple! This is your chance to make it up to me! Survive!"

S-shut up! B-bloody!

At the unknown name, the chunk of black armor on the demon's right arm suddenly started to rattle. The vambrace unfolded, turning into a spike that covered his hand completely. It was a sinister thorn that thirsted for blood, and thus, it bore the endearing name Bloodeater – or Bloody for short.

The worm, confident that it could take on the seemingly helpless demon, screeched in defiance and shot up towards the demon. But then, something happened the monster likely hadn't expected. Just in the moment the demon was about to disappear in its mouth, he gripped one of its long teeth, now dangling above its endless throat like on the edge of a cliff. Gulping, the demon looked up at the wall of flesh he was now surrounded by, and gore splattered about as he stabbed Bloodeater inside. As soon as the ominous thorn met the red, a slurping sound could be heard, and its blackness slowly turned a slight crimson. The worm screeched in pain, the demon swinging left and right like a pendulum.

You oversized bug! You like to hide beneath the earth? How about I help you hide forever?!

As if on cue, Bloodeater let out a burp, and the demon gripped on tightly as all the blood from the worm was redirected past his elbow. The beam of red cut a hole through the flesh of the worm on the other side, while the thrust sent its head careening to the left. The earth shook as the monster hit the earth, and another cloud of dust rose up. The traveler, having witnessed the spectacle from the outside, furiously clapped his hands as he walked over to the still twitching worm. He couldn't see the demon anywhere.

"What is he doing, quitting halfway through?" Like anyone with respect for the dying, the traveler stopped clapping and lifted his sword to end the misery of the worm. A flurry of silvery strikes cut through the air, and each of them parted the monster's sturdy carapace without resistance. Where the blade passed, it was like the worm itself was rewritten to never have existed in the first place, while everything else was left unscathed. But no matter how subtle the slashes may have been, their target itself still burst apart, and a huge wave of bile shot out of the open maw of the worm. A stinking fluid spread out over the plains and flushed out a cursing demon.

YOU BASTARD! I could have died!

"Died?" the traveler replied. "Not really, no." The demon, looking like a moving pile of slimy green, stood up and retracted Bloodeater into his vambrace before stomping over to him. Unfortunately, it wasn't only a funny sight but also stank horribly. "Please, watch your hygiene some more, disciple. You're already stalking me, you don't need to harass me with your smell as well."

S-stalking?! I only follow you around because I need you! B-but not that way, alright? And besides, there isn't anything here to clean this mess with in the first place! We are in the middle of nowhere!

At that, the demon suddenly got an idea, and a sadistic grin appeared under the slime as he got even closer to the traveler. The air around them quickly began to reek. "O-oh, my disciple, of course I didn't mean to inconvenience you. Why are you coming so close? Please stay away."

Oh, I don't think so. This, too, is your fault, so here, take a deep breath. Better get used to it.

"Nooooo!" Before the demon could get close enough to touch him, the traveler ran to avoid death by nose, while his stinky disciple followed to try and kill him as usual. For the rest of the day, they chased around each other and ahead, and internally, the demon felt a little happy. The bile of the worm seemed to be the perfect sunscreen for him.

After what would come to be called the Stinky Worm Incident, the traveler and the demon didn't encounter anything meaningful. The days of travel that followed afterwards were just like the first, a monotonous hike through an unchanging sea of dry green. The demon had always been confident in his own stamina, but he grew slightly anxious as dusk and dawn continued to line up without the traveler taking any breaks. Soon, he was forced to resort to the souls he had saved up for his Break Day to not risk starvation, and then, he even had to ration what little of them were left. Looking at the traveler's back the whole time was like torture for his increasing hunger, the soul inside so full of emotion, who could resent a little demon for wanting to take a bite? But fortunately, he wasn't so far gone that he couldn't control himself, which was partly caused by the bulla of the Queen and partly because of his growing suspicion that something wasn't quite right with the traveler. A human that could walk for days straight without a single break wasn't exactly normal, but if magic was added to the equation, many things became possible. It would explain why he had not been able to catch the traveler back in that little town, and who knew what else he didn't know about him. The thought alone made him feel queasy.

So that way, the traveler kept walking, and the demon kept following, always driven by the hope to be there the moment the traveler died. But the suns rose and sank, sank and rose while his strength drained, and his stash of souls turned slim. Then, at sunsdown of another day filled with rustling grass and numbing walks, the day a mountain range came into view to their left, the demon finally found his limit. He had been running on fumes for a few nights now, hoping for an imminent break: One more step, he told himself. Just one more step, and they would stop. But they never did.

Two strong, weak legs gave out, and the demon collapsed to his knees. The trampled grass between them looked just the same as the days before, and when the traveler turned around, it scrunched loudly beneath the heels of his boots. When the demon lifted his head and noticed his dark gaze, silhouette sharpened by the dregs of sun spilling past the mountain range, he finally understood.

Haha. So that's what you meant back then.

But although the demon laughed, his words rang hollow. Now everything made sense, and the answer was so easy: The thing in front of him was not human at all, or at least not anymore. That was the reason why he couldn't catch it back in the city, that was why it wasn't afraid of him, a demon, and that was the source of its endless endurance. And if it wasn't human, the being in front of him could just as well be anything. Maybe it was one of those things that could never be killed, would never die of old age, or could disappear out of his reach at any time. The demon silently pitied himself and his luck that had let him stumble upon something like it. After having been played with from the start, now he would be left behind in the middle of nowhere. And once that happened, his hunger would soon eat him up from the inside. As the demon realized all of this, the traveler stared at him while the suns continued their descent. Again, it seemed like a move to provoke him even more.

Come on! Go and leave… You have won.

But when the traveler heard the demon's defeated voice, saw him kneel in the dirt, pitiful and weak, the only thing he felt was happiness. This was such a special moment, a turning point in this story, but also a decision that *he* couldn't make. So he waited silently – until the demon eventually got angry.

LEAVE! Can't you let me keep the rest of my pride?! Am I *that* ridiculous!?

But the traveler kept up his silence. Just a little longer, he observed the demon who started to shiver, imagining a silent pressure the traveler seemed to exude. Perhaps, it was an instinctual response, with how similar this unknown being behaved to his superiors. His superiors… It was that thought that gave the demon an idea.

I know! Y-you know the Crimson Queen, right? Please, let her dissolve my contract so I can go back to the Den! I will do anything for you in return! Really, anything!

"Oh?" the traveler uttered, like he had just heard something surprising, and a beaming smile spread over his face. His plan had worked! As the traveler suddenly vanished, the demon found his head forced aside, and a mouth, dyed dangerous by the harsh shadows of the attacking night, nearly touched his pointy ears. "My disciple," someone purred into them, "I must say you gave a promising performance up till now." The grip on the demon's horns disappeared, and he looked up just in time to see a single tear roll down the traveler's face. "You are interesting! And naturally, I tend to stick with interesting things! What do you take me for? *A heartless monster?*" While the traveler chuckled at his own joke, the words still sank into the demon's mind, and when the traveler patted his perplexed shoulder, his whole body wobbled in relief. The demon was quite confused. The only thing he had to do was ask? Had it been that easy the whole time?

"Unfortunately!" the traveler suddenly was at his other ear, startling him from his thoughts. "I do not work for free!"

A-and what are you working for?!

At that, the traveler laughed another time, and the demon joined in, swept along by the silly atmosphere. Or, maybe, he just couldn't cope with all those sudden changes in the traveler's mood. It didn't matter if there was a price for the help of this being, it was completely alright. After all, this was how it always had been, in deals and throughout his whole life.

"Yes, let me show you my price." A parchment suddenly appeared in front of the demon, ink running together on its surface to form a short text. When he read it, he laughed even louder, more hysterical, before he suddenly fell silent. For a moment, the rustling grass around them stilled. This couldn't be.

The demon will receive passage to the Den of Sins in return for his obedience. For six complete cycles of the Milleniogram after his return, he will follow any orders, and until then, neither party will endanger one another, directly or indirectly.

It was a demon contract, but written by someone who wasn't a demon. He couldn't believe it.

W-who are you? How–

“You can sign the contract!” the traveler sang, his arms extending to an audience only he could see, “or you can rot!” The demon shut up. A contract between two demons actually wasn’t unusual, but he had never heard of anything else using them. “Time is ticking!”

With shaking hands, the demon shook off all his thoughts and lifted a single claw to place his sigil below the contract. While he would never agree to these outrageous conditions an other day, right now, he was left with no choice. Regardless of the price, this was the best chance he had to return to the things waiting for him in the Den.

As soon as the contract was signed, the traveler bowed with a smile, retreating a few steps while the parchment disappeared. “Now that we have taken care of that, my demon, let me ask you a simple question: Why do you think I would know the Crimson Queen?”

THE COLORLESS QUEEN

"Why do you think I would know the Crimson Queen?"

As soon as these words reached the ears of the demon, his expression flipped completely.

what, What, What?
Could you repeat that, please?

The traveler followed his request, but again, the demon couldn't understand. He didn't know the Crimson Queen although he had her bulla? No, if he didn't know her, that would mean–

YOU TRICKED ME! YOU FILTHY BASTARD!

Blinded by rage, he lunged at the traveler, but a jagged, crimson circle flashed up on his forehead and forced his body into the grassy earth. The contract wouldn't let him act on his need to vent on the traveler.

Ugh, you damn…

His face in the dirt, the demon heard the traveler dance up to his side before a small hand patted his back. "There, there, my demon. I didn't trick you at all. You won't attack me, and I will help you get back home. Isn't that what you wanted?"

AND HOW ARE YOU GOING TO DO THAT!?

"It's too late to care about that, isn't it?" the traveler chuckled. "Trust me, play along, and it will make things much easier for you." Although his casual tone only fueled the demon's anger, after staying on the ground for a while, he reluctantly admitted that he had a point. Now that their contract was signed, resistance was futile. He could only answer the question.

Everything is the fault of your damned bulla.

"Of this thing?" The traveler held out a hand, and the small metal ball appeared before the demon's eyes. "Why?"

A bulla, you dumbass, is something you don't simply hand out to strangers. It's proof of trust between carrier and owner, and the one you own belongs to the Crimson Queen, the savior of all demons. How did you get it if you don't even know this much?

The traveler remained silent for a moment. "I think… Maybe I just found it somewhere?"

Please. The Queen is the most mysterious of the Lords, you just don't *find* the belongings of such a

person lying around. If anything, and I really hope I'm wrong, you stole it from someone else.

It was a worrying thought, but the traveler simply couldn't remember. "How about you tell me what you know about her? Perhaps it will ring a bell?" The demon gave a tired sigh as he sat up, giving up the hope that anything could ever help this person.

Something is seriously wrong with you.

And yet, he slowly started to speak.

What the demon chose to share was a story so old most worlds existing back then were now less than faint memories. It was a time where there were no demons, and no angels either, a time in which all of them lived as one in Leysahrah, a round city flying in a sea of clouds. For millennia, the Leysahrians cared for the souls of the worlds from that shining bastion and acted as unseen helpers of their creators. But that harmony didn't last forever.

On the day the sun darkened over the city, the half of Leysahrah later known as the angels suddenly betrayed the rest, and half of their world was destroyed in the battle that followed. Its losers were driven out of their homeworld, from now on Leysahrians only in their memories, and became a drifting people. Doomed to be carried by the waves of the Eternal Sea and into worlds all across creation, the survivors abandoned their old secrecy and devoured all souls they encountered. In the process, chaos spread destruction, and many lives were lost.

However, not everywhere the survivors washed ashore were they met with equal resistance. A few worlds were unable to defend themselves and were lost to history. Others began to worship their invaders, falling to the allure of their power, but that, too, only prolonged their inevitable end. But among all of them, there was one world that was different. It was a barren place, devoid of every life and purpose, and when the first of the drifting landed on its shores, they quickly realized something: Here, there was nothing to fight against and thus nothing to feed on either. As more and more of the betrayed arrived on that single world, it didn't take a day until they began to fight each other. And who could resent them for it when, without souls, they were doomed to starve one after another.

This was how it went for a long time. Comrades that had stood side by side to protect each other fought until they forgot their shared past, and even those that remembered had no choice but to kill or die starving. And then, when their last lifeline, the flow of new arrivals, was about to dry up, even the future of those few seemed dire.

But not all former Leysahrians had washed up on the shores of that nightmare. And not all of those were spending their time killing everything they saw. Some were patient, curious and inquisitive, and while the rest of their people killed and died, they learned, until a single one of those moderate scholars found a way to part the Eternal Sea. By fate, or the will of the creators, she stumbled upon her lost brethren, and of course, she was horrified by what she saw: Her once proud people had been reduced to savage beasts, the faces of her old friends either eaten or branded by their suffering. The sight broke her heart, but using her outstanding genius, she found a solution to their problem. The hunger stilled. The fighting stopped, and so, her people revered her as their savior. For now, there was peace. She had saved them from their self-destruction. But the demons were not yet called demons, the angels not angels, and the Queen was not yet dyed crimson.

"How many are there today?" asked a smooth voice in a stuffy office, its owner sitting behind a desk bending under the stacks of documents placed on it. All of them were addressed to the person who had spoken, their appearance hidden by their work, but from the way even the rest of the room was drowning in paper, that wouldn't happen anytime soon. Between all the documents, however, and in front of the desk, knelt a single demon. He appeared a bit out of place between all the bureaucracy, and it was also strange that he was kneeling although the wall of documents on the desk hid the gaze of person on the other side completely. Or maybe it wasn't. After all, it was a matter of respect.

At the question, the demon looked up to answer, and the long, purple veil hanging from his horns shifted as if to hide his identity. "In quadrant one, its two million hundred-and-two thousand and forty-two. In quadrant two, its two million hundred-thirty-nine thousand and hundred-forty-four. Then, quadrant three, we have nine million three-hundred-one thousand and nine-hundred-eighty, while quadrant four is just one million five-hundred-forty-two and seven-hundred-sixty-one."

"All in all, that makes for a total of fifteen million eighty-five thousand and nine-hundred-twenty-seven demon casualties today." A pen scratched over paper as the person behind the desk jotted down the impassive numbers before giving a displeased noise.

"Quadrant three is still going through the roof compared to the others. Did you find anything regarding that matter yet?"

"Forgive me, my Queen… It appears Lord Gavrog knows very well how to hide his trails. Maybe we won't find anything at all."

The master of the kneeling demon, the Crimson Queen herself, couldn't help but sigh as she heard the news. "I need you to find proof. Assign everyone available to this matter if you have to, Tower, but give me something, *anything*, before the next Parley. Something is happening, and we have to find out what."

"Your wish is my command," the demon responded, and vanished as soon as her pen continued to write. The Queen had finished yet another report – but in the kind of Den she had created, the paperwork did never end.

When the demon ended his story, the traveler, now sitting in the grass in front of the demon, couldn't help but frown. "That's everything you know?" There was the slightest trace of disappointment in his voice. "This just sounds like fairy tales to me…"

Is that supposed to be an insult? This is a story taught to all demons from birth, so it's definitely true! Not like all those other rumors about the Queen!

"Other rumors?" the traveler asked. "So you *do* know more." The demon rolled his eyes, obviously considering it below him to list all of the rumors he mentioned.

I tell you, this is a waste of time.

"Humor me."

Ugh. Fine. Have you heard that the Crimson Queen is responsible for the first Harvest? Or that she tried to stop it? Or that *she* was the one who invented contracts? But no, that can't be true, because the Parley created them! Oh, and I almost

forgot: Purportedly, she is hiding under the bed of naughty children, so if I was you, I would be really careful the next time I go to sleep! On top of that, she–

"Alright, alright, stop!" the traveler eventually relented, which made the demon turn away with a satisfied snort. The honor of the Queen seemed to be quite the sensitive topic.

In place of silence, the cooler night winds swept through the grass around the demon until he sneaked a fresh peek at the traveler. Although his eyes were hidden by his hat, he was clearly staring at the bulla in his hands.

Did you remember something?

"Nope!" Giving up, the traveler shrugged it off and leaned back into the grass. "You should sleep now, demon. We still need to walk a while until we arrive at my goal."

Your goal? When *exactly* did you plan on bringing me back home?

A laugh was his reply. "Everything in due time, my demon, everything in due time. We don't want you to collapse again, do we?"

Was that supposed to be a joke? With empty eyes, the demon slumped down right where he sat, an ominous premonition in his mind. It didn't seem like his way back to the Den would find its end anytime soon.

A MUDDY ARRIVAL

The demon's rest ended all too soon. The stars faded, uncaring of his need to sleep, until the first sun spilled over the plains to stab him awake with its rays. His eyes opening with a grunt, and glancing around, he quickly noticed the criminal.

Why does this shitty world need two of those fucking suns? One is bad enough already.

In his drowsiness, he hadn't really expected an answer to his question, and yet, a voice spoke up right next to him. "I think the words you were searching for are good morning." The demon flinched, slowly turning his head before springing away when he saw who had been talking.

You!? My nightmare! Am I still dreaming?!

"No," the traveler replied with a grin, "you are quite awake." To confirm his statement, he suddenly poked the demon with his bindle, hard enough that it hurt through his tough scales.

Ouch! You are lying! It's just like in my dream!

The demon hurriedly tried to retreat, but the traveler jumped after him with an ominous laugh. "It seems you aren't tired anymore! You know what that means…" Scared, the demon retreated even farther. His legs were still tired and his hunger so bad it made his heart ache. He didn't want to.

Please don't.

"Back to walking!"

Another stab.

On this new day, with a contract of 'friendship' established between demon and traveler, absolutely nothing changed. The demon still had the very same food problem, and they kept walking like all the days before – although now, there was even less of a reason to. He complained multiple times that he could fly, but no matter how often he nagged the traveler, he didn't reveal their destination. With no choice, the demon continued to set one foot before the other. He walked and walked, and this way, he came to find a deep insight into the world: Walking was incredibly boring. They did it all the time and nothing happened, and now that he had *slightly* fewer worries on his mind, it nearly made him go insane. Even the pleasure from the soul he consumed behind the traveler's back couldn't lift his mood, way too little to still the painful hunger in his heart. It was like torture that he needed to be frugal – but relief finally was in sight.

Following their endless walking, around noon, the landscape finally began to change, and after the monotony of the plains, the demon was more elated at the sights than any other scenery before. Even if it was just to distract himself, he watched the mountains to their left grow closer, while the obnoxious grass below their feet finally fell back. It got colder and wetter, sandy dunes and scattered shrubbery now lining their way, and a fresh wind started blowing into their faces. Feeling the colder climate on his skin, the demon's mood worsened, only slightly improved by the clouds that blocked out the suns. While he had stared up at them, however, the traveler had stopped. He almost collided with his back.

Hey, can't you at least give me a war… ning…

From their vantage point, the highest dune of the beach, traveler and demon took in the wet plane of sand spread out below them. Its surface glittered slightly in the shafts of light piercing the clouds overhead, a sparkling band of stars that underlined the horizon. But the reason it appeared so bright, was the dark wall that rose up right behind it.

On the other side of the gleaming mudflat stood a cliff, stretching like a dark wall from the mountains on the left to vanish somewhere on the right. It was a breathtaking monument of nature, but despite its size and unmovable sturdiness, its surface had been destroyed long ago. The countless faint lines seen at the top split the rock straight to the bottom, and what remained of the former glory looked like rows of aged teeth, broken and derelict. Clearly, this was a place no normal person would step into. The traveler appreciated the view for a moment, finally they were there, but then, the demon suddenly got up into his face.

Is this it?! No more walking?!

Chuckling, he lowered his bindle from his shoulder and walked down the dune towards the mud proper. "No reason to be so happy about it! Welcome to the Cursed Coast, demon, the worst place in this whole world! Only the outcasts ever set foot here."

Oh, so it's a place that suits you very well?

"Yes, that's right!" the traveler agreed to his jibe. "But for you, that's true as well, isn't it?" Not waiting for an answer, the traveler stopped at the wet sand and stabbed his bindle deeply into it. The overly clichéd item suddenly split apart, disintegrating into countless shavings of wood and fabric. Slithering and rearranging, the thin ribbons started to mingle with the mud, forming a strange, bird-like creature from its mixture. Ugly, flightless, and with a big, fat body crowned by a tiny head, it stared at the traveler with hollow eyes. Especially with the piece of paper dangling around its neck, it looked just like an abandoned puppy.

What, by the tits of Ysel, is with that ugly bird?

“It’s not ugly,” the traveler chided his uncultured demon. “It’s our cute little guide. How else would we get through all this mud and to my contact on the cliffs?” But although the traveler called it cute, to the demon, said guide looked less like a bird and more like an accident. Stumbling with every step, it swayed left and right after the traveler turned it towards the mudflat, pecking at the wet sand ahead with every fall. The demon almost lost his mind as he watched: Never before had he seen something that was *so* damn slow.

That thing will bring us to the cliffs? Why can’t I just fly? It will take hours to get all this mud out of my claws!

“You can’t fly, demon, because even for free-spirited people like us, it’s sometimes necessary to follow protocol. Or how do you think people will react when a demon suddenly drops from the sky and randomly destroys a few doors?” At that reminder, the demon sheepishly scratched his cheek.

That just happened because that door was so flimsy.

“Yeah, I’m sure it was.” The traveler turned around, not believing him for a second. After all, he had opened said door as well – and it had not been flimsy. Ending their conversation, the traveler remained silent as they followed the bird into the wide mudflats. The demon reluctantly stomped after him, but as expected, the fine, wet sand grated between his claws as he sank into it way deeper than the traveler ever would. At first, he still told himself that they would arrive soon, but even after what felt like hours, the previously short distance to the cliffs seemed undiminished. The very same ponds and rivulets appeared ahead just to disappear behind them, almost like the sand was a wall that was supposed to keep them away forever.

Annoyed, the demon sprang across yet another stream of ice-cold water, careful not to get wet, and looked up. Suddenly, and without him noticing, they had arrived in front of the cliff, giving him a first impression of how enormous it really was. Its steep rock face stood so high and wide, he and the traveler had to look like ants in front of a giant, and in proportion, the faint cracks he had seen from afar had turned into oppressive, black cuts inside the rock. Staring up into one of them, the demon hesitated at the humid air wafting out from inside. After light, the thing he hated most was water, but when he looked around, the traveler was already about to disappear inside. Once more, the demon had to follow, and soon, they left behind the first black cut, taking one right angled bend after the other. Instead of a simple, broken cliff, this place seemed more like a labyrinth.

Are you sure this is a good idea?

The black forest growing on top of the cliffs creaked as the demon voiced his anxiety. No leaves were growing on its dead trees, only a white and silent fog that held off the light. What really worried him, however, was all the drooping kelp lying in the puddles they walked through. This place was obviously part of the ocean. He shouldn't be here.

"Don't worry, my demon!" the traveler replied cheerily. "We will be there soon, you only have to trust the script!" Despite the not very reassuring answer, the demon fell silent. He wouldn't get a normal one anyway.

Accompanied only by the rare creaking tree or flying bird above, they proceeded through the eerie corridors of the labyrinthine cliff. Although, all of them looked the same to the demon, there were those that were narrow and those that were high, sometimes short and sometimes endless. Even the traveler couldn't maintain his bearings under these circumstances, blindly following the bird that guided them. Somehow, the strange creature seemed to know exactly where to go, bending around corners and stumbling through crossings without delay. And then, when the path back was so twisted no one could remember, the ocean returned. At first, it was just a trickle, but one that swelled to a shallow stream until the icy water eventually reached the demon's ankles.

Will we be there soon? Did you plan to stay here forever?!

Rolling his eyes, the traveler turned around, something akin to annoyance appearing on his face for the first time. Rather than the water, it was his new demon who bothered him, completely destroying the atmosphere with his nagging! "If you really want to get out of here, instead of whining, be quiet and follow the bird!"

'If you really want to get out of here, be quiet and follow the bird!' Admit that we could have just flown from the start!

"I already explained to you why we didn't! Is it *so* hard to understand?!" But while the traveler was busy arguing with the demon, the bird that was supposed to guide them reached another junction. It looked left, then right into the corridors, hesitating for a single moment like a child crossing a street – a child blasted away by a rush of water suddenly flooding into the corridor. By the time the traveler whipped around, their guide had already been washed away without a trace. "Amazing!" he said and turned to the demon who watched with a shudder as the water rose to his knees. "Now you've gone and done it!"

Y-yes, what a pity. Can I fly to the top now?

"No! You stay right where you are!" Exasperated, the traveler started to call up the cliffs. He had not given up the chance that someone would notice them. "HELLOOOO?! ANYONE THEEERE?" his voice echoed up, disappearing among the trees as the water rose below them. "I'M SEARCHING FOR RAAKA, THE WITCH OF THE WATERS! POL-PHRABASH SENT ME!" Again, a few birds passed by over their heads, but no one answered.

Meanwhile, the demon stood in the ice-cold water rising by the second and glared silently at the traveler. Why was he so stubborn? From the start, flying would have been much quicker, so much easier! But just then, a quiet whisper reached his ears, almost like people stood above them, conversing in hushed voices. He was just about to call out to them when a shrill caw sounded down the cliffs.

"S-stop tampering with the aversion speeell, you nitwits! Weee're not falling for the same trick again! No one wants you Edgies here!"

"Right, right you are, Shanty! The Paperdoll will be furious! Iahaha!"

Finally, an answer. Visibly relieved, the traveler hurriedly patted down his drenched coat. "I came with a referral!" he called up the cliffs. "From Pol-Phrabash!" But although he checked all of his pockets twice, of said referral, there remained no trace, and only then did he remember that the important document had still been *inside* his bindle, around the neck of the very bird now drowning in the depths of the sea.

"I-Iaahahaa! A refeeerral he says? What are wee, Shanza? A fancy reestaurant?!"

"Yeah, your right, Shanty! Never heard of Poll-Grabass before either! Does that cunt as harassment?! Heeelp, harassment!"

While the aggravating voices yapped on, the traveler scratched his head. All of this seemed to be a big misunderstanding, or had his information been wrong? Or maybe, this was the sudden adversity for the protagonists?! “Listen up there, I just want to–”

“L-LEEAVE! The Edgiees must leeave!”

“Yeah, Shanty! Leave and drown, bitches! Iaahahaha!”

“L-le—ave!”
“Leave! And! Die! Suckers!”

Before he could reply, the traveler was suddenly lifted by the scruff of his neck. The demon had grabbed him, wings already on his back and enraged that someone planned to drown him in this water, this *icy* water!

HOW ABOUT I DROWN YOU INSTEAD!?

Just like that, his bat-like wings sprayed sparks as they shot up the narrow corridor and towards the annoying voices.

“G-gah! A-an attack! The Edgiees! ‘Zaza, put up the Wards, quickly!”

“Yeah, Shanty! Coming right uaaahhhp...”

Silence.

"...Shanty?"

"Y-yes, Shanza?"

"...I dropped them."

"W-whaaa?! Commencing retreeaaat! Reetre—eeeat!"

In an onslaught of hysterical shrieks and flapping wings, whoever was above the cliffs made a quick getaway. When the demon broke through the misty trees above, the forest was empty. "So much for being guests," the traveler commented dryly, still dangling from the demon's hand. He scoffed.

We weren't exactly welcome in the first place. Next time we find those shitheads, let's just punch them to death.

"Definitely not. You can still do that *after* I've found the Witch."

A promise is a promise.

"*Only* if it doesn't cause too many problems." The traveler understood the demon's anger. It wasn't like he enjoyed getting his clothes drenched or his script changed without an interesting way out, but right now, the Witch was more important – given that she, hopefully, existed. Who knew how many more lies he had been told? Wondering about that question, the traveler stayed silent until he noticed that the demon still hovered in place. He was still held in his extended hand like a kitten. "How about you let me down now?" At that, the demon looked down at him with an ominous grin.

As you command, m'lord.

"T-that's not what I meeaaaaant!" After the traveler broke through the branches of the misty trees, he landed hard on the top of the cliffs. The demon crashed down next to him not a moment later, clearly amused.

"Very funny. This can only be the fruit of my teachings." The demon choked on his laughter which made the traveler stand up with a grin. A black forest now surrounded them on all sides, its swaying branches like twisted hands gripping unmoving mist. Not exactly a calming sight.

Well, at least it's dry here!

Ignoring the demon with a sigh, the traveler headed where the wing flapping had disappeared into. Hopefully, there was someone around who didn't want to kill him on the spot, someone a little more fit to be talked to. His demon included.

THE VOICES

Searching the ground for any sign of the voices, traveler and demon proceeded through the mist-laden forest and along the chasms of the maze below. Seen from the top, its hallways divided the clifftop into neatly rectangular islands, the gaps running between them ranging from tiny to gaping abyss. Combined with the twisted branches crowding the forest, the chasms turned into treacherous traps filled with ocean water, and more than once, the traveler had to find another way around before the demon was so impatient he flew him over on his back – not that they really knew where they were going.

After yet another one of those strange crossings, the traveler was about to proceed when the demon suddenly stopped him.

Something's coming.

The words had barely formed in his mouth before a booming noise ripped through the forest in front of them. Splinters and trees flew through the air, and the traveler shielded his eyes as the demon took out his weapon. When the rain of wood ceded, and the traveler lowered his hands, he summoned his own sword when he saw what had happened. The forest, just now a confusing thicket of trees, had been ripped apart by an explosion, leaving an empty clearing in its wake. The mist was gone, showing a round patch of sky surrounded by the remaining trees, and in its center floated a strange sphere, a ball of bumpy glass distorting the image of everything behind. The demon and the traveler were still staring up at the strange sight together when the bubble suddenly burst, and a three-legged giant, completely encased in metal armor, crashed onto the top of the cliffs. Ignoring the cracking ground below, it charged forward, the dark visor of the cone helmet wrapping its head pointed right at the traveler. Judging from the ridiculously large hammer already swinging down on him, this wouldn't be the peaceful conversation he had sought – but just as the traveler completed that thought, the ground shook another time as the weapon smashed into his head. And just like that, the traveler was dead.

The giant snorted once, about to lift its hammer when it noticed something odd. Neither blood nor gore were sticking to the head of its weapon, just feathers that now flocked to its visor like a murder of angry crows. Confused, the giant tried to understand what was going on – when its second enemy, the one it hadn't examined yet, started to yell behind it.

HOW DARE YOU!? YOU KILLED HIM!

The demon was filled with rage as his own thorn-like weapon stabbed at the giant's back. Without that scatterbrained traveler, how was he supposed to get home?! Expressing his frustration, sparks sprayed up as Bloodeater's tip collided with the giant's hammer.

Despite the feathers hindering its sight, it had blocked the demon's strike – in no small part because of his tendency to yell.

"A-ah! Look at theem, 'Za, fighting our mighty warrior! One of them is already gone!"

"Yeah, yeah, right you are, Shanty! I tell you, those Edgies already regret that they stole our Wards and attacked us! Cowardly!"

"I-Iaahaha! Yes, I can't wait to dance on their bodies once theey're dead! All of them that is!"

"Iahahaaa! Right you are!"

Ignoring the familiar voices jeering on in the background, the demon backed off from the giant after his attack had failed, not wanting to risk a hit from its deadly hammer. Using that opportunity, the hunk of metal removed the feathers blocking its sight, scrutinizing his second opponent for the first time. "Huh." A confused sound echoed from its helmet, its deep, baffled voice tinny through the layers of armor. "Since when does the Edge employ *your* ilk as its soldiers?" Hearing that justified question, the two lookouts in the distance abruptly shut their traps, which made the armor-clad giant turn around with an eerie creak. It was about to demand an answer from them when the touch of a fragile sword suddenly pierced through its armor, the thin blade caressing its spine like a feather.

“The Edge employing demons?” the traveler, alive and well, replied to the giant’s question. “You really should come up with better jokes. Why would you even think that?” The blackness inside the armor was silent for a moment, maybe just as baffled as the demon who stood a few steps away. Or perhaps, the three-legged warrior was simply afraid that the blade would pierce his back. “Actually,” the traveler continued, “I clearly stated that I have a recommendation from Pol-Phrabash.”

“What do you want?” the giant scoffed eventually, trying his utmost not to move.

“Oh, you know.” The fountain blade stroked teasingly across his skin. “I’m looking for the Witch of the Waters. I was told that I could find her here.”

“You heard that from Pol?” The giant sounded annoyed. “That old geezer never learned to respect our privacy. Whatever. You’re obviously not from the Edge. Why don’t we stop fighting for now?”

“Fine by me~!” With that, the tingling disappeared from the giant’s back, but when he turned around, the traveler was gone, leaving behind only a bunch of feathers trailing onto the broken earth. Waiting a short way behind them, however, was the source of the mysterious voices, a pair of strange beings not quite alive in the classical sense. Instead of flesh and blood, their bodies were twigs stuffed in a cage of ribs, growing desiccated, clawed wings and the legs of birds. With their heads lowered, the two Animata, lifeless objects with consciousness, cowered in the dirt, shivering so intensely that their baggy pants fluttered left and right. But unfortunately, the giant knew them far too well to fall for their act.

"Do you have anything to say for yourselves?" he said angrily, and the twins looked up, revealing the only way they could be distinguished from one another. Carved with different expressions, a wooden mask sat on their respective faces, that of the left eternally surprised, while the right one's was upside down and drooped tiredly. For once, it was droopy eye who answered first.

"We didn't know, Yarok, didn't know! And they really *attacked us, right, Shanty?!"*

"Y-yeah, listen to Shanza, oh mighty one! We neeearly died!"

But the pressure radiating from the giant only increased at their excuses. "You nearly died? And what about the Wards you received to keep any enemies away?!" At that, the two Animata shared a silent look.

"S-Shanza droppeed them!"
"Shanty dropped them!"

"What?! You traitor!"

"R-right back at you, son of a bitch!"

"That makes you one too!"

"W-who carees?!"

A hammer smashed down between the bickering twins and forcefully ended their budding argument. Scared, they looked at Yarok who bent down, gulping when his pointed helmet cast an ominous shadow onto their heads. "If you don't want to end up as kindling, you better listen to me, you little shits."

You're alive?

The demon flinched when the traveler suddenly stepped from a small storm of feathers that disappeared as quickly as it had arrived. "Of course I am." He stopped in front of the demon, giving his still lifted vambrace a few playful pats. "Did you really think that little hammer could kill me? How disappointing." While the demon stared at him, the traveler gave a dramatic sigh. "My disciple, it seems you still have much to learn."

But *how* did you evade that thing?! I saw it crush you! Even the ground split!

Realizing his demon's lack of basic knowledge, the traveler rolled his eyes. "Surely, you have heard of translocation?"

Of course I have! But that's impossible!

Naturally, a demon, one of the few races known to travel freely between the worlds, had heard of this rare kind of magic. In essence, it denoted all spells that instantly moved objects from one place to another, but usually, it could only be used to travel *between* worlds – and not inside of them.

"No," the traveler corrected, "it isn't impossible. Not for me, and, didn't they do the same too?" While saying so, he pointed at the giant named Yarok, who was busy shouting at the two Animata a short distance away. Indeed, the strange sphere that had appeared earlier was quite similar to what the demon now tried to deny.

Huh, you're... right? But if you could do this the whole time, why did I have to carry you over half of this maze? Did you want to fly with me that badly?

Obviously, being abused as transportation didn't sit quite right with the demon, but the traveler didn't even try to deny it. "Yes, you are completely right, I just wanted to fly on you. After all, don't we all seek for a strong back to carry us over the cliffs of life? I just couldn't resist when I saw yours." His soft chuckle felt like a punch into the demon's speechless face – and unfortunately, Yarok interrupted them before he could find a good retort. Behind the approaching giant, the Animata still cowered on the ground, their twigs slightly more ruffled than before.

"I guess I have to apologize to you," Yarok conceded after stopping in front of them. "We're stretched a bit thin right now, otherwise the likes of Shanty and Shanza would have never received you." It sounded like an honest apology, almost like the giant was actually a merchant, but the traveler didn't care how sincere it was. He only wanted to know if the Witch of the Waters was living in this place – so quickly asked for her.

"I'm afraid meeting her isn't possible at the moment," Yarok replied, his helmet swaying wearily in denial. "You could wait until our situation turns for the better, but that's not going to be the case anytime soon." The traveler frowned when he heard that. While he was relieved that his information about the Witch hadn't been wrong in the end, Yarok's words were simply to strange.

"What could keep her so busy she can't even take a break for a moment?" The giant sighed in response, slumping down for a single instant.

"Maybe it's better if I show you. Why don't you come along?" Waving at them to follow, Yarok turned around and approached the Animata who sprang to their clawed feet when they saw him approach. The way they were now expectantly staring up at the giant made it seem like the pitiful state they showed just a second ago had only been an act the whole time. "Quit dawdling and get out the markers, you idiots! And don't you dare fuck it up again!" With eager nods, Shanty and Shanza hurriedly rummaged through the twigs inside their open ribcages, pulling out two wands with translucent gems on their tops. Although they looked quite important, that impression only lasted up to the point where they started to perform a silly dance with them.

Can I punch them to death now?

At the demon's quiet whisper, the traveler hurriedly shook his head. "I think that would cause quite a lot of trouble right now. You can wait." Grumbling, the demon reluctantly agreed. Those two ugly dolls had tried attacking him first, so this would clearly be a case of self-defense. And he urgently needed a few souls…

Shanty and Shanza, blissfully ignorant that they had come this close to dying, were now skipping circles around their small group, dancing wildly until waves of light spread out from the wands they held. Like billowing curtains, a bright cocoon quickly formed around all of them, and only when the outside had been veiled completely did the Animata stop, clacking their wands together in a carefully studied pose.

"One hop baaack!"

"C-Coming right up!"

With that, the bright wall imploded, sucked into nothing with the sound of a vacuum cleaner throttling on a blanket. The people who had been inside of it were now gone, leaving behind only a fresh and lonely clearing. The forest returned to silence as it looked on. Where had they disappeared to?

TROUBLED MAZE

Seen from the sky, the cliffs and the glimmering mudflats surrounding it may have seemed endless as they ran along a good part of the continent, but they, too, had an end. Far south from where the traveler and the demon had entered the plane of sand, the waves covering it stopped disappearing, and even the towering cliffs, higher here than in the north, abruptly cut off. Over time, many of its square segments had been swallowed by the tides, but on the highest of those that remained rose a large tent, right next to the precipice. The winds howled fiercely around it, threatening to rip it off the peak, but despite that, it was silent behind its thin walls. As if denying the threat of the storm, the crisp sound of a turning page rang out again and again, the big tome it belonged to illuminated only by a crystal resting in the mechanical hand of its reader.

"Hmmm."

A thoughtful sound could be heard, followed by scratches over paper as a long, white beard turned to the next page. The tiny man hunched over the tome carefully read another sentence before looking over to the center of the tent where an ancient machine reflected in the thick lenses of his triple glasses. It was a mysterious contraption, its towering parts arranged in an embrace, and the small man scratched his egg-like head as he thought about how to repair it. An idea had just formed in his mind, his spiraling ears twitching in excitement, when a buzzing noise suddenly came from the depths of the machine.

"Hm!"

A frantic noise later, the Porker had jumped from the stool he had been standing on, almost tripping over his wide robe in the process. It was important that he hurried, for with each second he lost, the machine in the center of the tent whirred more to life, got more out of control. Barely a second passed until he pulled lever after lever, dial after dial, but so close to mystery, control was a relative term. Even though he knew from experience what settings he had to make, the machine was just too old, too ancient, and as one part after another broke under pressure, he was left with no choice but to work quicker. Pulling levers with one arm, he extended his mechanical one before its hand suddenly unfolded, splitting into a forest of fingers that reached for the rest of the machine. Each of the thin limbs could be called a full hand in its own right and instantly began to swap out breaking parts for new ones before they could explode. His valiant fight continued until a ding rang out, and the arms of the strange machine suddenly pulled a group of people from the void in their embrace. Silence followed, and then, as if this was the last thing it would ever do, the machine simply fell apart. "Hmm!!!" The sounds of the pitiful Porker swept through the sweat and grime, but he was merely able to watch on as one piece fell onto the next, damaging even more in the process. Staring at the now broken heap of metal, he gave a despondent sigh, already imagining all the repairs required to fix this, but frustrated as he may have been, the people who had just appeared in the center of the tent didn't care a bit about his plight.

The traveler looked around as soon as they arrived, curious about how someone had managed to replicate his own skill, but Yarok herded them towards the exit before he had time to ask any questions. They had just passed the Porker when he suddenly looked up from the remains of his machine, gesturing fiercely with his metal hand. Instead of a mouth, it was the clinking of its countless fingers that interlocked to create a grating voice. "I really hope it was worth it!" he said, clearly angry at Yarok or maybe just frustrated. "Ports will be closed until I manage to patch up this mess!" The giant nodded once in acknowledgment, leaving the Porker snorting at his obvious lack of respect. But instead of complaining, it was way more productive to start fetching some spare parts – at least until he noticed something else. "A demon?" His scathing voice trailed after their group. "Did you sink this far already?"

"You don't have to worry, Professor." Yarok reached for the flap of the tent. "They are just guests." With that, the entrance was opened and they stepped outside, the demon leaving a last teasing wave before it shut for good. Alone again, a frown appeared on the

Porker's large forehead. And it was deeper than any frown before.

After the tent released their group, they found themselves at the edge of a cliff stabbing into the darkening sky. Around them was just blank stone cluttered with rock pillars howling in the winds, and without the straight chasms cutting between them, nothing would have revealed that this was still part of the same cliff they had been on a moment earlier. Curious, the traveler took a step forward, right up to the edge, where a spotty blanket of gray clouds came into view, moving slowly in front of a dull blue ocean. This really was a high place.

"If you would follow me," Yarok said impatiently, paying no mind to the view of the clouds below and heading left to a narrow pathway leading along the edge. At this height, even flying beings would have difficulties braving the winds, so everyone stuck to the opposite wall as much as possible. Even Shanty and Shanza, who trailed after the rest, were no exception. A few rocks scattered across the edge as Yarok bent around a corner where the narrow path opened up to a slightly wider stretch of rock. Hanging from its right and into the air were a row of strange platforms, in turn leading to a small shack at their end. It was a shaky construction, built on scaffolds gripping into bare rock, and those questionable supports seemed to be the only thing holding the complex in place. From the looks of it, it would be no surprise if it collapsed any moment, but Yarok stepped onto the walkway without a care. Stomping past the swaying platforms and towards the small shack, he rapped his fist against its roof. The poor building shook dangerously, and shortly after, a small door was opened in its side, Yarok exchanging a few words before he returned to lead the rest of them onto one of the platforms. Despite its rickety impression, it carried their weight as they all took position around the strange barrel in the platform's center. By the time they were done, the door of the small shack burst open once more, and from it, a flock of ducks, no, of small, beaked apes rushed out, each of them carrying three wooden poles. There was one for each arm, and one for the hand at the end of their tails. The Duck Duck Apes, or Dudupes for short, looked almost cute as they loudly whirled the sticks above their round teddy ears, and wherever the wood collided, the clicking sounds mingled with the hollering quacks coming from their beaks. It was a literal flood of them, Dudupes pouring from every opening of the shack, more than had any right to fit inside – and soon, every last one of them had gathered in the center of their already well filled platform. Slowly, the horde of Dudupes quieted down, glancing nervously at the demon while one of their gray-haired elders climbed onto the mysterious barrel. His long beard fluttered in the storm as he shouted up at Yarok over the wind.

"The whole way down, standard speed?!"

"Make it double, if you would." Grimacing, the gray Dudupe turned around, his underlings already clambering over each other to lock the poles into the barrel he stood on.

"Get going, guys! Slavedriver speed it is! And one, two, three!"

"Quack!"

"QUICKER, SCUM! One, two, three!"

"Quack! Quack!"

"One, two, three..."

And with each quack, the Dudupes circled once more around the barrel, turning the winch inside to lower the platform bit by bit. Thanks to their unending efforts, the ledge over their heads quickly fell away, fading to an endless wall of rock that protected their backs from the biting winds. They had just cleared the milky layer of clouds when Yarok spoke up, pointing to the ocean spreading everywhere below them. "You wanted to know what keeps the Witch so busy?" he said to the traveler. "Then look closely at those damned mountains."

Mountains? The traveler blinked the last cloud from his eyes before raising his gaze, and on the newly uncovered ground, not quite at the horizon, he indeed found a mountain range. The demon, too, followed Yarok's words, but more to put his hungering gaze onto something other than the Dudupes laboring at the winch behind him.

At first, they didn't notice anything unusual. The mountains were just mountains below the darkening night, harboring a single group of dim lights, a city, at their foot. The traveler was just about to inquire what exactly they were looking for, but then a few of the lights suddenly split off to slowly set out for the open sea. The demon was the first to recognize them.

Ships?

He was indeed correct in his observation. As their platform lowered and the lights came closer, they turned from dim dots into plain wooden vessels, fielding white sails of a simple make. They didn't look like anything special, but in exchange for that, they were easily built, repaired, and expendable. And despite their plainness, what made these ships threatening wasn't their quality, but the crest fluttering proudly on their storm-filled sails. It was a shield, formed by six arrows radiating from a circle. The traveler couldn't quite believe it.

"Ha! Are you at war? With The Vanguard of World's Edge?" A snort echoed from Yarok's visor, although the traveler's reaction was understandable. The Edge was an influential organization that had once spread through all of the worlds of the Eternal Sea, and even today, no one in his right mind would want to start a fight with them. Yarok didn't even disagree with that sentiment, however…

"Of course, we didn't *choose* to pick a fight with them. It's just that–" his giant helmet bowed closer, words a whisper echoing inside, "–not everyone living in the Cursed Coast is an Original of this world." Hearing that, the traveler hummed thoughtfully, his eyes still trained on the armada closing in below. Originals and Others were old terms that had been coined by the Edge, for although they were a diverse group of people, they also held a *slight* bias against those who traveled between worlds. They called them Otherworldlers, Others for short, and their opposite were Originals. Yes, like so many others, that matter had gone terribly wrong in the end, and the traveler couldn't help but comment on this unlucky circumstance.

"How strange of them to attack you unprovoked, regardless of the Others that may have gathered here. The Vanguard branch in this world must be quite extreme." This was likely just a case of bad luck, after all, almost everything could be found within the endless Eternal Sea. But Yarok didn't seem to feel the same way.

"Ha! Aren't Edgies the same everywhere? We never did anything to them, but suddenly, it's Otherworldlers here, Otherworldlers there… We just helped a few of them, and suddenly, the Edge came to destroy us." The traveler frowned. This was not how he remembered things to be. "But don't worry," Yarok continued with a meaningful nod down towards the ships. "We do know how to defend ourselves."

Hearing that, the traveler's gaze flew back to the ships, but what Yarok was so proud of was unnoticeable at first, starting deep in the dark ocean with a single speck of light. As the spark rose up, it turned into two, then six, then a hundred until a whole swarm of icy fireflies surfaced on the now glowing waves. The traveler squinted his eyes, and with their platform closer to the waves than ever, he recognized those lights as runes, symbols used in magic. Thousands upon thousands of them were swimming on the sea, their soft shine illuminating the clouds overhead just like they painted fear into the soldiers on board. At the first sign of this grand magic, the fleet slowed, and alarm bells rang from deck to deck. Although they were seemingly prepared, not just sailing to their deaths, whatever countermeasures the Edge took were obviously fruitless. Unimpeded, the runes gathered, watery tentacles sprouting into the air to slam into the ships, and the first screams started to echo through the night as their hulls burst open like ripe fruit, contradicted by the sound of cheering somewhere below them.

The demon gulped at the massacre taking place so close to his eyes. Although the ships were quite a distance away, he could clearly imagine all the souls freed out there, just as clearly as he could imagine the icy horror of the waves. But while the demon shivered, the traveler's eyes seemed to sparkle at the beauty of the spell, not even considering that the Edge had perhaps been right to consider this place dangerous.

Watching as the ships were destroyed one after another, their platform continued to descend, and only when there was nothing to fight against did the light fade from the sea, the darkening tentacles of the spell splashing back into the water. The night had returned to normal, and without the spotty moonslight revealing the casualties, the whole event could as well have been an illusion.

Suddenly, Yarok laughed, which pulled the traveler's eyes away from the blue graveyard. "Quite awe-inspiring, isn't it? As long as we have the spells of the Witch, we can defend against everything – and we have to. If the Edgies win here, it would be much easier for them to take the rest of the maze, and all of us would need to flee. You should understand now that you have seen this: The Witch has her own duties to consider."

"I can't meet with her?" the traveler said, slightly dejected as he spoke to himself, and Yarok firmly shook his head.

"No, you can't. This kind of spells take a heavy toll, so she sleeps most of her days to recover. Those damned Edgies have been trying to wear us down ever since, and it's working. We can't allow her any distractions." Silence lowered onto the platform after that final statement, only broken by the quacks of the Dudupes and the sighs of the demon. Inside, though, the traveler had his own opinion on this matter. Regardless of whether he was allowed to see the Witch or not, he would still see her. It wasn't just a matter of finding the author of his note anymore, now, she also seemed like an interesting person. Why did she try to resist so fiercely when it was clear the Edge, with all its endless resources, would be the winner in the end? Why were they always trying to sacrifice themselves?

Drumming his fingers against the wooden railing in front of him, the traveler waited for the platform to arrive on the surface. He was dying to meet the Witch. Or at least as close to it as he could get.

GIANT FANS

The platform arrived on the ground with a crash, and two Dudupes sprang forward to pull away the railing in front of the traveler. Stretching on past it and over the water was a wooden pier, and the Dudupes' unspoken pleas told them to leave as soon as possible. The way they kept glancing nervously at the demon while everyone left, they likely were afraid of him, and when the platform rose back into the sky, it did so even quicker than it had arrived.

Following the pier below, Yarok stepped onto the bleak island extending on its other side. It was a narrow gathering of rock so thin that the waves could be seen left and right, but also long enough to appear to have no end. Square boulders were scattered all around, and Yarok continued along a well used path between them. On the way, they walked past countless pools of water, used thick slabs of stone to pass over winding channels, their walls sharp and angular despite the constant tides dancing inside of them. The longer they walked up the strip of island, the fiercer the water gushing left and right seemed to get. The waves kept rushing in from the ocean, spraying up the channel walls and into the sky where it fell down as airy screens of water. The demon cursed every time one of them went down on him, and if not for his new contract with the traveler, he would have turned around this very instant. The time stretched as they endured the cold wetness until the rocks finally spat them out in front of a strange building. It was high and wide, a dark cutout against the rising stars, and made up of twisting tendrils thicker than even Yarok was high. Rather than a building, it reminded them more of a plant that simply grew here at the end of the island, a part of its tendrils spilling over the rock and into the sea. On a second look, the green coils even sprouted inside of the waves, forming a glinting forest of thorns that kept every ship away.

"Welcome to Merai, shadiest bastion against the Edge." Lowering his gaze from the piled up vines, the traveler saw Yarok standing in a gaping hole leading though them. It was the entrance to a tunnel, deserted and empty, and past its inky black spread a city, its tents dotted with the lights of a hundred lamps. Compared to the wealthy Caldette, it was a crowded and makeshift place of cloth and shacks, squeezed tightly side by side. There was so little space, the unpaved streets could barely separate the buildings around them, and even the square stone pillars towering up here and there were covered in tents. The air smelled strange, smoky and dirty, and despite Yarok's grand introduction, the traveler suddenly felt reminded of a refugee camp. Surely, he had to have seen a few of them before, for they were common as sand with worlds and whatnot dying every day. Overcrowded, dirty, and chaotic, crammed with hopeless people and crime severe – that's how he remembered them to be, leaving an uncomfortable

feeling lingering in his mind. But as Yarok led them on through the tiny streets, he slowly realized that his expectations didn't fit. While it could be considered strange that most of the people still on the streets were actually children, the surprising part was the missing worry on their faces. Not even at the sight of the demon did they show fear, maybe because Yarok was walking ahead of him, or maybe due to the small pendants they clasped tightly in protection. Whatever the case, something wasn't normal about this place. Confused, the traveler looked around another time, now seeing what his bias had him ignore previously. Compared to other refugee camps, the streets of this one were not abhorrently dirty, its tents orderly and clean enough that it almost reminded him of a proper city. And the reason that set apart this camp from the others? He already had a premonition.
Slowly, their group continued through the knotted streets until they opened up to a small square. It was the first free spot of ground they had come across, and at its far end stood a tent distinctly larger than the others. Seeing it, Yarok turned around and spoke, "Please wait here for a moment. I have to take care of somethin–"

"Siiir Yaarok!" a high voice suddenly interrupted him. "Weelcooome ba—ck!" Behind Yarok, a fluttering shape burst out of the large tent, weightlessly skipping across the square and towards them. The human woman, it appeared, wore clothes suited more for an antiquated noble ball, her dress so frilly and decorated that it was a mystery how it could hold its dome-like shape under their weight. Without exception, all the fabric she wore was white, or rather off-white, matching her skin and the color of her hair. In the blink of an eye, the woman had arrived in front of Yarok and spun once underneath her umbrella. Only now that she was closer, though, did it become clear that she wasn't human. From the clothes on her skin, the skin itself, and up to the umbrella in her hands, the woman was a single, elaborate origami, folded from a thousand sheets of paper. At the same time, she was so lifelike that a single step of distance was enough to blur the faint lines left between her pages, turning her into an almost perfect human replica. Almost? Because the most eccentric thing about her was her head which was completely plain, a simple and blocky thing missing any details it ought to carry. In place of the graceful face one would expect, a mere drawing was displayed on its flat surface, moving and changing like its real counterpart. The moment the traveler saw those traits, he knew what this woman was, a Papersnip, an elusive race of paper creatures that counted few among its members. Theirs was a species that could take many forms and shapes, but no matter how their contents made them look, they all were just paper. And as such, there were two things all Papersnips ought to avoid like the plague: Fire and water. Slowly, the traveler held up a hand to make sure, but he could still feel the slight spray of water the tides scattered all over the island. Why would any Papersnip be in a place this wet?

The traveler was so distracted by all the odd things he found in this place that he hadn't noticed how strange the demon acted since they had entered the city. Even now, he was blankly staring into the distance, counting numbers to distract himself, but no one paid any attention to it. Especially the Papersnip's flat eyes were only fixed on Yarok, so much so that she was unable to acknowledge the rest of them. "Sir Yarok!" she nearly squeaked at his pointed helmet while the drawing of her face turned into the image of happiness. "You are back! Tell me, what was it? Why were you suddenly called away?! What happened?" She asked and questioned, questioned and asked, but before Yarok even had the chance to answer, the woman finally noticed the rest of them.

"Oh," she uttered, her tone instantly sobering up as soon as she spotted Shanty and Shanza. "Oh," her voice turned cold when her gaze reached the demon, and she flinched when she saw the traveler. "I understand now." While it wasn't quite clear what she understood, her words sounded quite admonishing as she returned to ignoring everyone but the giant in front of her. "Do not forget that you still owe me a few battle stories. And the armors! You wanted to show me some armors too!" Her pleading expression returned to her face along with her pleas, seemingly softening Yarok's heart.

"There is no reason to rush, Lady Alwera. Not everything is about war, you know? At least let me take care of our guests first." At his tinny words, the Papersnip was finally reminded of her rudeness, causing her to sheepishly clear her throat and take a step back.

"You are completely right," she admitted, embarrassed that her passion for battles had carried her away once again. "But, Sir Yarok, there really is no need to be so formal. I already told you to call me Ellie. El-lie!"

"O-of course, E-Ellie. I will *definitely* remember next time." While Yarok was obviously flustered at her straightforwardness, Alwera's face swapped out for one filled with suspicion. This wasn't the first time he had promised that.

"If you say so, it has to be true," she eventually replied before slowly turning to leave. "If you would excuse me." Her eyes met the traveler's for a moment, and she jumped into the air, opening her umbrella to catch the wind. Swaying left and right like an autumn leaf, she vanished behind the tents standing around the square, gone just as quickly as she had arrived. While everyone else was still busy staring after her, the traveler glanced around, but no one seemed to have seen the words that had appeared on Alwera's face when she had looked at him. *We have to talk tonight. I will find you.* It certainly was a nice trick, but talk about what and why, he had no idea.

With Alwera finally gone, a relieved sigh escaped from Yarok's mouth, and he spoke up once more. "As I was about to say, I have something to take care of. Please wait here for a moment." The giant left, and without Alwera around to stop him, he quickly disappeared into the large tent on the far side of the square. When he stepped back out shortly after, two rough looking soldiers came charging past him, instantly grabbing Shanty and Shanza to drag them off to who knows where. Although they had expected this, they didn't leave silently.

"Y-Yarok, onee more chancee!"

"Please!"

But the giant mercilessly ignored them, and even the few people peeking out of their tents went right back to sleep when they saw that it was just Shanty and Shanza. Yarok followed them with his gaze for a while, seemingly in a good mood as their wails lost themselves in the city. Eventually, he turned around. "As a sign of our friendship, and to make up for you meeting those two, we will provide you one of our tents, free of charge! What do you say?"

It was a surprising offer, but the traveler happily agreed. Otherwise, he would have to search for a place to stay on his own, and it was quite late already. Seeing him nod, Yarok led them out of the square and once more between the tents. On the way, they passed by a larger version of the figurine everyone they crossed seemed to carry with them. It was crudely made and looked like a small child with a mop for hair, and this time, the traveler instantly asked what it was supposed to display before something could interrupt him.

"This is Raaka!" Yarok laughed in reply, explaining as he continued through the streets. "Can't you recognize the Witch you're searching for?" When he noticed the traveler's doubtful stare, his laugh got even louder. "Before you ask: No, of course she does *not* look that way. Those statues are so ugly because they were made by the people living here." Hearing that, the traveler was amazed.

"So the Witch is like an idol? Did she manage to be so adored only because she is protecting this island?"

"It's not just that," Yarok denied. "Raaka is the one we… owe the existence of this camp to. It was she who led the very first trek of refugees onto this world, and she who helped them build a new life up from the ground. The people simply show their thankfulness every way they can."

Scrutinizing another statue passing to their left, the traveler asked himself how there could be such a benevolent person. He knew how hard it could be to play that kind of role. "But enough about that." Yarok suddenly stopped right in the middle of a street that looked like all the others they had passed until now. Tents were lined up left and right, their insides either empty or sleeping soundly, and after turning around, Yarok pointed at one of them. "This is where you stay. In case you have any questions, don't worry – someone will come to take care of you tomorrow." With that, the giant walked away, leaving a confused traveler watching him vanish into the twisted streets. Why hadn't he said a single word about his demon…? His demon? Turning on the spot, the traveler looked up and down the empty alley. His demon was gone. Suddenly, a cold, lonely breeze howled past their tent, playing sadly with the traveler's coat until he decided to head inside. A demon, he thought, should be able to take care of himself, and anyway, there were more important matters to think about. Like the Papersnip that was coming to meet him, or his sleep. Those were his honest thoughts, but only because he had forgotten something important: Even demons had their demons, and one of them was called hunger.

MIDNIGHT DEALINGS

The tent-filled streets flew by as the demon ran through the night, jumped off, and rose above the sleeping city after calling his wings. Their flapping, wild and uncontrolled, was swallowed by the stormy gales sweeping over the island, causing him to nearly fall from the sky multiple times. But the unpredictable wind was not the main reason he struggled so hard. It was all the fault of this damned city. After having gone hungry for so many days, the amount of people gathered here was like a buffet to a starving man, a sea of souls where even a single one was impossible to resist. Currently, he was so sensitive to their smell that he couldn't focus properly on the way ahead, and while he struggled to keep control, he didn't really pay attention to where the gales were dragging him.

The next time the demon looked around, the city had started to fall away, and he was almost above the icy depths of the ocean. Hurriedly, he struggled to a stop before he could shoot out over the blue-gray waves, but in his weakened state, it turned out more like a plunge than a descent. Rocks and gravel sprayed through the air as his body dug a furrow into the shore, coming to a stop right before the sloshing waves. The wall of vines in the background, the demon looked around the shore, his breath heavy and his heart hurting. Where was he? What did he want to do again?

"Hey!" A high voice suddenly came from the square rocks around him. "I think a perwson just fell fwrom the sky!" Hearing the voice closing in, the demon sprang up and ducked low, hungrily looking around. Who was talking? With blurry eyes, he turned on the spot until a small shape rounded a nearby boulder, and as soon as he saw its soul, he lunged at the unknown person, pressing them up against a nearby rock. His claws had already closed around their head when something hit his foot with a wooden clatter, causing him to look downwards with a hiss. There, on the gravel at his feet, laid a small crutch.

At the sight, the demon's mind suddenly cleared, and he ripped up his head, glaring at the small and frightened puppy dangling from his hands. It was a Canid child, a mix of human and dog, and the left foot of this one clearly stuck out at an unnatural angle. It was a cripple. Hissing, the demon let go and retreated, ignoring his hunger that begged him to pounce on this piece of food. He growled, the words he spoke to the Canid on the ground sounding much hoarser than usual.

Leave. Don't… come back.

The puppy, visibly afraid, nodded hastily before clasping his crutch to crawl away, and only when it had disappeared completely did the demon dare to move again. This had been close. If he really wanted to return to the Den, he couldn't afford to give in to hunger. *Uphold Control,* that was the first tenet all demons had to follow, and any of its transgressors would quickly receive the most cruel punishment. With a shiver, he remembered the cages displayed by Notoriety Relations , and tried to take a soul from the stash in his chest. But to his dismay, only a single one of them was left. It was a weak and fragile light, the pink color of its feelers indicating that it was close to poisonous. Ignoring the risk, his hands fumbled greedily as they crammed the soul down his mouth, and while it stilled his hunger, the familiar high didn't follow. It was just that weak of a soul.

Disappointed, relieved, and stupefied, the demon lowered his hands to stare at them with a sad expression. He was out of souls. Finally realizing that, he looked around, his eyes wandering along the strip of shore in an onset of desperation. He urgently needed more food, but at the same time, he couldn't go around and randomly kill people to get it. The reason for that was called *Justify Evil,* the second tenet, which was, in practice, as simple as the first: Without a summoner's tasks as the reason for his deeds, he was now forbidden to commit crimes. It was a rule that, in a way, was the cause of his current predicament, and yet, the demon didn't couldn't bring himself to resent it. After all, like everyone else, he didn't want another war against the angels…

Still slightly lost, he continued to look around the shore when his red eyes suddenly caught on something half buried beneath the gravel. It was a body, rotten and bloated with age, but the crest of the Edge was still visible on what little of its clothes hadn't been stolen. Staring at it, the demon suddenly got an idea, and the gravel crunched between his claws as he moved forward once more. As he walked between the square rocks ahead, more and more washed up corpses appeared, apparently left as fertilizer for the vines. At each body, he stopped for a moment, examining them closely. Maybe, with the recent casualties of the Edge, he could find a few souls still clinging to this side of the veil. Choosing to bet on that hope, he started a long search down the shore.

Across the vine wall and on the other side of the city, the traveler was waiting in the tent Yarok had assigned to them. While it was a considerably spacious room, its round walls only held two beds standing to each side of the entrance, one of which the traveler was currently lying on. Surrounded by darkness, he stared at the note he had already studied back in Caldette, reminiscing in the face of his goal. If only the Witch could help him find its author…

Crumpled once more, the note went flying through the tent, vanishing as he moved his gaze up to the cloth ceiling. How much longer would he have to wait? Right as that thought passed his mind, a rustling sound reached his ears, and he turned on top of his bed to face it. There, on the other side of the tent, a flat sheet of paper slowly shoved underneath the wall.

He stared at it for a second before the flattened being suddenly unfolded, and without as much as a greeting, Lady Alwera stood inside his tent. She didn't even knock. "Don't you know how to use the front door?" the traveler asked her. "What if I had taken a bath?"

Seemingly surprised, Alwera froze, baffled by his casual reaction. "You are different from what I imagined," she muttered thoughtfully, almost as if this was some grand scientific observation.

"What did you imagine?"

"Naturally, someone more serious. Like your colleagues."

"Colleagues? I do not have any '*colleagues*.'"

"Oh? Perhaps I was wrong. You are quite serious." Was that supposed to be a joke? Staring at Alwera, the traveler blinked a few times until the Papersnip suddenly remembered who she was talking to. "How rude of me." She gave an elegant curtsy. "Allow me to introduce myself. My name is Alwera, but they call me the Fairstress, Overseer of Conflicts. What, if I may ask, is the reason that brings you to these shores, Constant Forgetful?"

Hearing her familiar way of address, the traveler sat up, slightly confused. As far as he could remember, he didn't know this person. Did he forget something important again? "Sure you are not confusing me with someone?"

Smiling, Alwera sat down on the bed across from him when she saw there were no chairs. "Do not worry. It is just how I call you internally, with no one knowing your *real* name. Do you not like it?" She seemed a bit sulky. "At least *I* think it has a nice ring to it: The Constant Forgetful who lives a hundred lives without remember–"

"*Stop it,*" the traveler hissed, and Alwera closed her mouth as he held his head in pain. Fortunately, she courteously waited until he looked back up at her. "I assume this is not the first time we've met?" But despite his harsh tone, Alwera seemed to find the question funny.

"Oh no, it is. I am simply someone who likes to know who to watch out for. As we Papersnips say, 'knowledge is power,' not that we have ever made anything of it." Slightly relieved to hear that, the traveler calmed down, but still retained some of his concerns. Was this person a stalker? Because if they had never met before… "How impressive that you would recognize me so quickly then. But your little title appears outdated. Those times are over."

"Really?" Intrigued, Alwera casually pulled out a small, black book, scribbling something inside without him being able to see. "How generous of you to tell me." As her book shut, the traveler just shrugged in response, and silence overcame the tent. Alwera somehow seemed distracted.

"…Did you only come to stir up the past?"

"Ah! N-No, not at all!" She finally snapped out of her thoughts. "I wanted to meet with you because of your business with Raaka." Hearing this, the traveler raised his brows.

"That is why you are here? Are you sure?" Alwera had arranged this meeting the moment he stepped into this city, a time where she couldn't have known that he searched for the Witch. Therefore, this couldn't be the real reason she had wanted to come see him, but she simply ignored his comment.

"You have to know that I am a *close friend* of Raaka, yes, the only one who is allowed to see her." She seemed quite proud of that fact, but her voice suddenly soured as she continued. "Because I know exactly *how much* everyone here cares about her, its also obvious that they would never let you, a stranger, meet her… But that does not need to stand in your way. Whatever you need from Raaka, I can mediate. You know, one hand washes the other? Figuratively, of course. Please do not wash my hand." Having presented her offer, the drawing that was Alwera's face redrew to become an adorable smile, but unlike with Yarok, its cuteness simply bounced off the traveler.

"And what exactly do I need to do to 'wash' your hands?" Alwera smiled at the question.

"Obviously, that depends on what *you* want from *her*."

The traveler sighed, slightly reluctant to reveal more than necessary to this strange Papersnip, but she likely wouldn't trust him otherwise. "You have to know, before this whole forgetting, as you call it, started, I had a few friends I lost touch with. Now, there were a few new… developments, and I have to search for them. Nothing more, nothing less." Alwera's eyes narrowed at his vague explanation before starting to wave the book in her hands.

"Who are those friends you speak of? Maybe I know them?" To her disappointment, the traveler only answered with a thin smile until she finally stowed away her notes. "I hope they are not in *this* world at least," she added grumpily. "Otherwise, you would have already found them."

"You're right about that." It seemed Alwera had already deduced what he needed from the Witch. In order to find something lost, a mage could resort to a spell of search. In theory, it was an easy type of magic, but in practice, its difficulty increased along with its range. While many practitioners could find something they lost within their own homes, it was something else entirely to find something that was lost across the worlds. For these cases, the Eternal Sea became an almost insurmountable problem. "But that's exactly why I'm here," the traveler continued in a meaningful tone. "I was told by someone that the Witch could help me anyway."

"Is that so?" Alwera wondered out loud. "Maybe. I think I will need to ask her first."

"You don't know? I thought you were close friends?"

"We are! We are friends! But that does not imply that we tell each other everything, right?!" Clearing his throat at Alwera's fierce reaction, he quickly glossed over the topic.

"I guess so. But, just assuming you're really able to convince the Witch to help me, what is it you want in return?" Snorting, Alwera leaned forward and held up a hand. "I want two favors." She held up two fingers. "First, you and *that demon* of yours have to help me escape."

"Escape?" The traveler was confused. "Speaking from how you talked with Yarok, it looked like you enjoyed this place." And indeed, back in the square, Alwera had appeared quite attached to the giant. Had all of that been just a front?

"So what?" she said behind the back of her apparent friend. "That has nothing to do with how much I want to stay here! I hate this island! It is wet, it is boring, and all those ridiculous security measures! Without them, I would have taken Raaka away long ago." But this confused him even more. What kind of security measures could restrain a Witch who could destroy a whole fleet? It didn't make sense no matter how he looked at it, although he didn't complain. It was quite convenient for him this way.

"I will help you escape. And the second favor?"

"The second? Oh, so good that you ask." Alwera grinned, wider than any organic being could. "It is a secret." Although he quickly tried to protest, Alwera didn't budge. "Take it or leave it." Annoyed, the traveler fell into sullen silence. These were the worst conditions he had heard in a long time, but taking her offer was still the best option. How frustrating it was that he had to be so careful.

"...Don't make me regret it too much, please?"

"Oh, why should I?" Alwera happily rose from the bed she sat on. "We have an agreement. I will confirm everything with Raaka and give you her answer tomorrow." Her curtsy was quick and elegant, and before he could add anything, she folded up, vanishing the way she came. While her satisfied smile made him slightly uncomfortable about this meeting, those were troubles for the future. With a sigh, the traveler pulled the hat over his eyes and fell back into his bed. With a little luck, there would finally be some good news tomorrow.

Back on the island's shore, gravel scattered up a flat rock as the demon slid down its surface and onto the ground. Hours had passed since the start of his search, hours which had exhausted him more than they should, and the results hadn't helped much either in improving his mood. The string of bodies he had been following the whole time had suddenly cut off, leaving him with only the two tiny souls he had found up to this point, as well as the company of the last corpse sitting right next to him. Had too much time passed since those soldiers died, or was he just more suited to fighting than this kind of work? With a questioning gaze, the demon turned to the body right next to him.

What do you think?

...

Of course, it didn't deign to give an answer. Whatever the case, with so little food, he would barely last another day. Giving a dispirited sigh, he leaned back until his head hit the rock behind him. His burning eyes seemed dim and weak, not at all like his usual self as they stared at the moonslit ocean. The ocean. While it was something he couldn't stand physically, he had always been fond of the endless play of its waves. It was such an alien sight, so fascinatingly different from the scorching heat he had been stuck in most of his life; the tunnels, the rules, and the hierarchy of the Den. Back home, it was always a constant struggle for food or recognition, and all of them just played their parts in the sacred machine of their society. *Follow the Protocol,* that was the third and final tenet all demons knew, but not one all were able to follow. Automatically, he had to think back to the cripple he had seen a while ago. For like in every machine, the useless parts…

At least the waves were beautiful tonight.

A moment passed in which the demon's mind remained blank, only thankfulness for his position as a Hand remaining. It was only luck that he had the luxury of being here today while so many others were stuck forever inside the Den. After a while, his square face tilted towards the starry sky, and he observed its shifting lights, wondering if he would ever manage to return. Was everything still alright back there? The birds soon started to circle above, scavenging for the remains of the battle just like himself, and although he observed them closely, they didn't have an answer either. But then, something suddenly fell from between their flock and hit right into the center of his eye.

Ugh! Are you serious?!

Cursing, he rubbed his face while the birds above croaked out mocking laughs. At first, he thought they had shat on him, but then, he noticed that it had only been a small, gray stone, now resting in his lap. Angry, didn't he already have enough problems, the demon prepared to hurl the pebble away before he lowered his hand to take a closer look. It was just a gray, eye-sized stone, maybe a bit too round but still perfectly ordinary. At least that was how it appeared at first. But why did it have a soul?

The demon pondered as he stared at the tiny octopus, its stubby tentacles clinging to the rock. Of course, his first thought was to use it as food, but he wasn't sure what would happen if he ate a soul that glowed white, something he had never heard of before. It was just as inexplicable as the translocation ability of his new master, and yet it was right here, in front of his eyes. Maybe, he truly knew nothing about the world…

In a rush of anger, he jumped to his feet and suddenly kicked the corpse next to him with all his might. Naturally, its rotten neck was far too weak to resist the sudden attack, and a head went flying through the night, landing with a satisfying thud as he turned around. He had no time for useless riddles, so he calmed himself but still remained slightly angry for some reason. Confused by his own feelings, he didn't even question why he could store the stone in his chest like any other soul, his mind already turning to the corpses waiting for him ahead. He really needed to find more food…

Somewhere in the south of the camp, a large shape entered the command tent and stepped up to the round table standing inside. A single lantern rested on its surface, but its light was only perfunctory, for it only darkened the shadows around it. Hidden inside the inky black stood a mysterious person with nothing betraying their identity, nothing, except their angry voice. "What were you thinking!" the shadow yelled at the larger shape as soon as it entered. "You brought a demon here without my permission?! Are you insane?!" They already had enough trouble with the Edge, and now this!

"P-Please, Commander. Listen to me first! This demon can be incredibly useful for us!" While the tone of the large shape was incredibly sincere, the shadow behind the table snorted in response to that unlikely statement.

"Useful?! This better not be an excuse!" Relieved, the large shape towered closer and whispered something into the shadow's ears until a grin spread in the darkness across the table. "Perhaps you're right. That was some quick thinking you did there. Maybe, just maybe, if this really can get us some breathing room, I *might* even think about your discharge." At that, the large shape bowed deeply and left, when the shadow inside suddenly called after them. "Don't disappoint me again." Nodding, the large shape clenched its fists, the ominous night swallowing them whole. With the plan officially approved, the only thing left was to start.

A GLIMPSE OF THE PAST

His eyes appearing from the night, the demon left the gravel behind, moving up a vine and along the wooden pier built on top of it. Although he had merely wanted to continue his search, instead of more corpses, he had found some kind of harbor. Devastated, he looked around the thicket of piers built on the vines all around him, but at this hour, they were empty and deserted. In hindsight, maybe he should have expected that he wouldn't be successful, considering that, since the beginning of this cursed mission, everything he started went awry.

Dispirited, he walked on without really watching his steps, the piers creaking below him until a tunnel in the wall of vines led him back into the city. With his recent meal, the souls sleeping inside the dark tents were inaudible once again, and with nothing interrupting his thoughts about how to get more food, the demon proceeded deeper and deeper into the twisted streets. Slowly, the alleys turned dirtier until even the shadows seemed to crawl with shady dealings, and it was at that time that he suddenly realized that he was lost. Before he could think of doing anything about it, however, a heavy blanket suddenly muffled his mind, a strange feeling that not his hunger was responsible for. Confused, he tried to understand what was happening, to escape from the unknown enemy attacking him, and while he stumbled forward and away, a row of lit tents came into view ahead. Their open fronts, spanned up to form leaky roofs against the constant rain, held crude counters and stools, and only the worst type of people was still clinging to them at this time. So when the demon stumbled by, his tail and limbs flashing up in the strips of light falling out from the tents, most of them were too deep in their tankards to notice – all of them, except one, who was too drunk or simply too fed up to care.

"Ey, you squeak scum!" a slurring voice oinked at the demon, interrupted by squeaks. "What are ya doin' in dis ciddy?" Along with the words, a drunk Spig stumbled away from one of the counters and headed towards the demon. It was a creature resembling an upright walking pig, but with a much bigger tail and another pair of hoofed arms below the first. Because of all the liquor, his four arms and his tail were swaying like a willow in the wind, the fluttering cloth of his threadbare shirt swaying along with them. Judging from the stains covering it and the extra holes ripped for his extra arms, he had to be quite poor, so maybe the drinks were not the only reason he decided to vent his anger here. "It is all your fault!" he yelled. "Without you, the Edgies squeak wouldn't hate us so much!"

Shouting and slurring, the Spig stepped in the way of the demon, but the reaction he got was not as expected. Moving like a sleepwalker trapped in a dream, the demon didn't react to his voice and roughly pushed the Spig out of the way. With an outraged grunt, he crashed into the muddy street, his beady pig eyes still fixed on the demon who simply walked on. He was obviously not taken seriously! Struggling to his hooves, he was about to follow when a few people hurried closer to hold him back. "Let me go!" he yelled into the worried faces of his friends, pushing them away to storm after the filth that had humiliated him. Wobbling, ahead and around a corner, he didn't really notice just how dark and lonely the alley was he suddenly found himself in. There, darkness against the shifting stars, leaned the back of that shitty monster, its arms braced against a nearby tent. Right now, it didn't look threatening at all. Those stories were obviously fake.

"Answer me, why are you here?! No one wants you here!" the Spig shouted, no, vented his bitterness at the abomination, everything so that he could feel a little better. But it still had the gall to ignore him. Stumbling closer, he was about to extend a hoof to prod the frozen silhouette – but he wasn't meant to get what he wanted. His world suddenly spun over, and two scorching eyes, one red, one blue, filled his whole view.

What? My lady? Is this a gift?

Who cares! Screw everything and just take it!

How thoughtful…

Wait a moment, no, what–

The Spig's ears suddenly gave out as the distorted voices drilled into his skull, and his body went numb, not that he had the time to care anymore. The next moment, his head was twisted from his shoulders, and the demon lifted it high, his two-colored eyes fixed at the crimson light of salvation stuck to its side. Relief was so close, he only had to rip out the soul and stuff it down his maw – but that, too, was something never meant to happen. A dull sound rang out between the tents of the narrow alley, and suddenly, everything went black.

In a strange dream, a world burned, a feast for violet flames that were the absolute end. In their wake, forests, cities, and even oceans were consumed, left as statues made of ash with cracks pulling through their surface. As the fire swept through the land, everything fell into silence – except a single place where screams echoed from within them. They were noisy screams, anguished screams, and they all came from a crying man, strangely unhurt by the flames around him and yet in pain. The reason, however, was simple: Inside his mind clashed millions of memories all at once.

By the time the victors had buried the losers, the man's thoughts finally came to a rest. The world he had lived in peacefully just seconds before had burned down to the bones, and with nothing to consume, the fire, too, had vanished. Now, there were only ashes below his knees and statues around him, leaving the man the only spot of color in a wide, gray plane. Still confused, he remained rooted, as one with the cracks around him, until he finally noticed the piece of paper buried between his knees. Picking it up with shaky hands, he saw the short message written on it, and as he read and reread, anguished voices started to appear. Maybe they came from the mouths of the incinerated, hissing at him from their cremains:

"It's your fault!" *"You did this!"*
"You said this wouldn't happen anymore!"
"So why did this happen?!"

But the man, hopeful once more, laughed at their questions. It was a sudden and clear laugh, the kind that freed people from an old burden. The last time they tried, everything went wrong, but this was the kind of second chance he had wished for since then. The perfect story, on the perfect stage, to live what he couldn't write anymore. Therefore, as the mouths in the ash hissed on and raised the curtains once more, the man lifted his arms to the now black sky. As he shouted up into its emptiness, he gripped the note tightly, crumpling it with his hands. He was so, so thankful, so "Thank you," he said. "Thank you–"

Mary.

As the name appeared, it brought the dream to someplace else. Into a different world, to a different time, to the eyes of someone he had long been estranged from. But the same wasn't true for the sight they were seeing. Not many were left he could still remember so clearly. Like a bittersweet painting shrouded in thick mist, the scene only reached up to the borders of the grass on the left and the river on the right, framing the tree in between. Below its leaves, there was a small boy who held a notebook on his lap and, right next to him, a girl rolling around in the lush grass.

It was summer.

"If we find it, you could write an amaaazing story! You could be *sooo* famous!" While the girl spoke, she continued to roll left and right, trying to catch the gaze of the boy with her sparkling eyes. Each time, green stalks flew everywhere, but the boy ignored her antics as he stubbornly wrote into his notepad.

"This again, Mary?"

"The adventurers I met said it's all real! And veeery old, and all old things are true, aren't they?"

"No, they aren't! Why would you believe adventurers anyway?!" the boy shouted, tired of leading the same discussion again and again. "This is just a waste of time, Mary, so stop thinking about it. A myth is just a myth, and no matter how hard you try, you will never find nor prove it!" As the words left the mouth of the boy, he gasped, but it was too late. In response to his challenge, Mary sprang to her feet with a big grin, pointing at him who remained sitting on the ground.

"Haha, just wait!" she said as the boy looked up to her determination. The light around her edges was blinding, and her index finger booped his nose without leaving a chance to evade. "I will show you all!" Her laughter rang like bells in his ears, their sound drowning out her image with light. How happy she had been back then.

Shooting up in his bed, the traveler brought up his hand and retraced her touch as the dream clung to his lids. Around him, soft light filtered through the worn parts of the cloth walls of his tent, shrouding his back as he thought about what he had seen. The last time he had dreamt… he couldn't even remember it, so why had this chunk of the past come back to haunt him? Was it the fault of Alwera's blabbering, or something else entirely? With a frown, he lowered his hand, now noticing the buzz out in the streets for the first time. There was so much noise, it made him feel like his very tent had suddenly become the loudest place in the whole city – and now that he thought about it, maybe this was the reason it had been empty in the first place. Cursing at Yarok, Alwera, and the working populace outside, the traveler stood up and stretched. The rest of the tent was empty, without a trace of his demon to be seen, but he didn't worry. What was the worst that could happen? With that, he put on his hat and left.

Out on the street, he squinted at the blinding strip of sky between the tents before a loud crowd came into view. Moving around him, flashes of limbs could be seen, attached to people who had the most various shapes. There were humans and humanoids, fluid and jagged things crawling or walking past him, some mixed with animals, covered in shell, or fur, or skin. As he stood in the middle of the street, his hat was nearly skewered by a horn, then almost blown away by a pair of wings before he quickly managed to catch it. During daylight, the streets became filled with a colorful mix of races, and although it may have seemed strange at first, it fit this place where people from all across creation gathered in their plight. Therefore, it wasn't their appearance the traveler's gaze was now fixed on.

Behind the people that clotted his sight was a host of restaurants and bars that seemingly appeared overnight. Not a single one of the narrow gaps between the tents was left empty, filled up by stalls that fit them like the pieces of a puzzle. Crowds and groups of people were standing next to them, eating and bartering in the clouds of smell while their chattering blended into the background. The closest of these stands was currently selling tasty-looking mystery-skewers to a tired looking sounder of Spigs, and those very skewers were what the traveler was staring at. Deciding to buy some, he tried to hand some money to the owner of the stall, but he only received a doubtful stare in response. Unfortunately, it seemed like the people of this island had a completely different kind of currency.

Longingly staring at the Spigs next to him, who were already scarfing down their breakfast, the traveler was already considering delivering them from their burden, but before he could, someone suddenly waved at him from one of the nearby tents. But who could it be?

Entering through the open front of said tent and past the counter at the side, the traveler stopped in front of a rickety table set up with a few others to form a small restaurant. Perched on an equally shaky stool next to the table sat a Minotaur, a human with the head and legs of a bull. Its huge body and horns were way too big for the cramped tent, making him, who was still waving dumbly, look quite ridiculous. The traveler was sure he had never seen him before. Well, as sure as he could be…

"Oh my, why are you standing there like an idiot?! Sit down already!" The Minotaur spoke up with a deep rumble befitting the image of their belligerent race, but unfit the polite words it had spoken. Holding back a laugh, he nodded at the strange invitation, his decision in no way influenced by the steaming pasties that stood right next to him on the table. Definitely not.

"You can eat them if you want. There were left ov–" The Minotaur's words got stuck in his throat when the pasties were suddenly gone, only a faint trace of crumbs remaining around the traveler's mouth.

"I hope you don't expect me to pay for this." At his shameless comment, the Minotaur put a hand to the bridge of his muzzle and suppressed a sigh. "I came to talk about the Witch," he said instead, trying to get this over with.

"The Witch? What about her?" The traveler retorted like he didn't know what the Minotaur meant. After all, they were strangers, and while it was certainly nice to receive free breakfast, the first date was a bit too early to talk about such personal things. In response, the Minotaur rolled his eyes and put out a hand, showing off his rough palm and the empty piece of paper resting in its center. The traveler took a look, but nothing was written on it, so he could only raise his gaze in confusion. Was this supposed to tell him something?

"Please, stop being stupid," the Minotaur pleaded, massaging his temple. The traveler looked back down at the hand of his breakfast giver, then back up, then, back at the hand. One more time, he was sure, and the Minotaur would crush his own head with the pressure of his massage. Wasn't this... beginning to get fun?

"ARE YOU KIDDING ME!? WHAT ARE YOU, A CHILD?!!" the Minotaur shouted angrily through the small shop, and the other customers around them fell silent with accusing stares. But the bull just huffed their looks aside and annoyedly pushed his large hand into the traveler's face. So close to the paper it held, he finally understood that it was actually part of the hand itself – and now, it even carried a short sentence, for extra stupid people: *I am Alwera, you shithead.*

"Ah!" he exclaimed, prompting the Minotaur to finally pull back his hand. "Now that you mention it, you do look quite similar." Hearing that, Alwera's Minotaur disguise visibly deflated. What had she been thinking trying to get help from this being? It was obviously far more dangerous than she had thought – for her sanity, that is.

While Alwera was recovering from the traveler's antics, he silently admired the quality of her disguise. Was it a glamour spell that made her look this way? What else could she turn into? Magic was always so fascinating, although he couldn't use it…

Taking up the steaming cup next to the now empty plate, he studied Alwera. "So? What did she say? The Witch?"

Hearing his question, Alwera weakly lifted her Minotaur head. "Well… She *is* able to perform the spell you need, but there are a few prerequisites. First, of course, an item from the 'friends' you seek."

The traveler nodded. This much was normal for any search spell, and naturally, he had already prepared said item. The note he had found fit the bill perfectly. "On top of that," Alwera continued, "she needs to use a special Rune Matrix to cast it."

"You sound like that's a problem?" The traveler knit his brows. "Shouldn't she be able to draw it herself?" After all, *Rune Matrix* was just a fancy word for a certain arrangement of runes, which most spells consisted of. He didn't mind waiting a few days until the Witch finished her preparations. At least that was what he thought while taking a casual sip from his cup, but then, Alwera replied.

"Unfortunately, Raaka said that the formations for *this* spell are… special. They require the star charts stored in the Keyseekers' Archae, like the one she studied at, but she lost access to them when she left."

Suddenly, a drink was spat out, showering down on Alwera and drenching her from head to toe. "The Archa she *studied* at?" the traveler shouted, just as disturbed as Alwera was by the wave of tea hitting her paper body – although it simply rolled off her. "This bastard!" the traveler continued to rant. "Pol-Phrabash never told me about this!" Following his shouts, the restaurant grew quiet once more, but now it was the traveler's turn to be stared at by the other guests. Not that he cared much either.

What Alwera had told him just now was a big problem. The reason he had been searching for the Witch in the first place was that Pol told him she could perform his search without involving the Keyseekers but… He had been deceived. So much for good news.

"Why is she part of the Keyseekers!" he lamented, and Alwera answered after quickly drying herself.

"She *was* part of them. As I said, she only studied there, and besides, what is your issue with the Keyseekers anyway? Why dislike an organization that is only interested in the pursuit of more knowledge? And on top of that, they offer important services for little money."

"Don't even try to start with this! If I could ask them for help, I wouldn't have needed your Witch in the first place!" The traveler crossed his arms and looked away, his face sullen below his hat, and Alwera let out a sigh.

"Oh, well, if you hate them that much, we won't be able to help you after all." With that, she stood up to leave but quickly found her arm grabbed by the traveler.

"The Witch only needs the star charts, right? No one said anything about taking the front door." His tone was serious, although his words were insane.

"*What?*" Alwera's mouth fell open, her rumbling voice becoming a whisper as she leaned in over the table. "Are you crazy?! In the first place, Raaka would never agree, and who knows what would happen if you were to be discovered?! You–"

"Don't worry." Her string of objections was stopped quite casually, and the traveler leaned back on his stool. If there was no way around the Keyseekers, then he had no choice but to integrate them into his plans. "Simply don't tell the Witch about the shady parts, and I will take care of convincing her once the time comes." But despite his reassurances, Alwera kept up her silent stare, at least until he reminded her of something in a hushed voice. "I thought you wanted to bring the Witch out of here? Wasn't she the reason you wanted to meet me in the first place?" Alwera flinched.

"How do you know?"

"Please. I am insane, not stupid."

Slowly, very slowly, Alwera sat down again. If the mess she was in hadn't been so deep, she would have never asked the Forgetful for help in the first place, so ignoring this would be easy in comparison. And if the Forgetful planned something too outrageous, Raaka would never agree anyway. "Alright," she eventually admitted. "But remember, I will not do anything to help you with this insanity! Remember it!"

"Yes, yes, I sure will!" The traveler grinned broadly, toasting the future and splashing ample amounts of tea straight at Alwera's face. If he hadn't continued right afterwards, she would have certainly lost it right then and there. "So tell me. What's the plan to get you out of here?"

MERCIFUL, CRUEL WITCH

While the traveler and Alwera talked about their escape, the people outside the tent were like waves that washed around the food stalls of the city. By the time they had finally decided on a plan, those waves slowly started to recede, and Alwera left the restaurant on her own to take care of her preparations. Everyone respectfully made way when she stepped outside, her crude Minotaur looks making people avoid as well as forget her. After all, no one would remember someone who looked like just another laborer returning to his work.

For a while, Alwera used the masses as cover until she cleared the restaurants and fled into an empty side street. The way she imitated a Minotaur all the while was so convincing that even the traveler had been fooled by it, but now that she was alone again, the large body she wore turned back into paper. It was a bizarre sight, a white giant crammed into the dirty back alley, and it only got stranger when a ripple suddenly sprang forth from the Minotaur's head. Where the wave passed down along his skin, the pages he was built of folded away into their archives and revealed the fragile woman who hid beneath.

Alwera, having removed her disguise, opened her parasol and returned to the streets. While the amount of people walking there had visibly reduced by now, it was suddenly way harder to get past them. The reason? Where Alwera passed, everyone started to whisper in her wake or swarm her like fleas that had spotted a comfy fur. They begged for this and asked for that, but no matter how desperate they tried to appear, Alwera ignored all of them. People didn't mean anything to her who just wanted to witness conflict, and never had she fulfilled a single of their requests. So why were they still so persistent?

In a way, it was the fault of the Witch. It was Raaka's nature to help everyone she met, and just by being her acquaintance, Alwera was thought to be the same. Or maybe, some people were simply too desperate to see the truth. Shaking her head, Alwera walked on and ignored everyone equally. If not for the stormy weather, she would have simply flown towards the south of the camp instead of walking there in the first place.

After clearing another mass of solicitors, a wall came up in front of her, and its sight drove away the last annoyances trailing her steps. It was a stone wall, higher than even her Minotaur form, and hidden behind lay the military district. The heavily guarded gate ahead was the only way to access it, but no one stopped Alwera as she continued through and into what appeared like a different world. Here, there was no sign of any tents, just flat buildings of wood and stone and streets so clean you could eat from them. Alwera was sick of it all, but she didn't need to endure much longer. For today was the day they would finally escape! That was why she had come here after speaking with the Forgetful, because the first step towards their escape was now right in front of her.

Stepping past more soldiers, Alwera arrived in front of a flat and unadorned wooden building. Unlike many of the other barracks, it was designed with privacy in mind, just large enough to hold two people. As she opened the door of that very building and entered the short hallway beyond, she found an empty hallway with two doors waiting at its end. One of them led to her own room, and the other… She knocked softly, but no one answered. Although Alwera could still remember the better days, filled with laughter and cheerfulness, this place had now become like a silent grave. It was the fault of The Edge.

The mute door creaked eerily as Alwera opened it, and a storm of feelings flew across her face so fast that it had passed as soon as she stepped through. On the other side was a small room occupied by a canopy bed, and its curtains billowed playfully around Alwera as she stopped at its side. There, on the mattress, she was; a small girl, gray like the ocean and with hair the glowing feelers of sea anemones. Along with her drooping ears that glowed much the same way, the twinkling strands framed a set of exhausted features. She had two huge eyes, broad lips, a nose that didn't narrow at the bridge, and Alwera studied them all as she slowly sat down at her side, the soft mattress barely denting under her lightness. As she sat there, like always, she watched the pained sleep of the girl, and like always, she didn't like the rings she saw below her eyes, even deeper than she remembered. To those who knew nothing of magic, the girl sleeping inside the bed may have seemed completely fine, but in truth, this was Raaka, the Witch of the Waters – and she danced at the edge of death.

Sitting next to her protégé, Alwera spent a few moments in silence before finally trying to wake her. While Raaka needed all rest she could get, there was no time to waste anymore. "Raaka," Alwera called her, but there was no answer. "*Raaka,*" she repeated more firmly and shook gently at soft shoulders. "Wake up, please. I know you are tired, but we have to talk."

Raaka, however, didn't wake up at all. Instead of opening her eyes, she merely shifted in her sleep, gripping one of Alwera's paper arms to curl around it like a cat. "Ellie?" she mumbled, and yet didn't wake. Like always, getting her out of her dreams was a truly difficult task – but Alwera had come prepared.

"Raaakaaa," she said in a teasing tone as she took out a bag filled with pasties. "Look what I have brought youu~" Dangling from Alwera's hand, the delicious smell emitting from the pasties seeped into Raaka's dreams, and finally, two amber eyes opened to look at her.

"Oh…!" Raaka said as she blinked blearily. "Hi, Ellie, what are you– *wow! FOOD!*" At once, Alwera's arm, which had been lovingly embraced until now, was tossed away like trash, and at the same time, the bag with food was ripped from her hands. "Oh, my food!" Raaka shouted, holding the pasties into the air like a precious artifact. "How I missed your tastiness! A-and thank you too, Ellie!"

While Raaka was busy praising the food, Alwera's hand that had held it now hovered quite lonelily in the air – she wasn't angry, however. In the first place, Papersnips couldn't eat like the flesh-dwelling races, and even if that were different, she would have gladly endured some hunger to see Raaka munch on the pasties. Like a little squirrel, a broad smile shone between Raaka's stuffed cheeks as she ate, and seeing her obvious happiness made Alwera happy as well. It was the proof that her charge had recovered from her dark past, and now, she encountered everyone she met with cheerfulness and kindness. While Alwera admired this friendliness, it also caused her to worry. What had happened to them on this island was evidence that Raaka had not only recovered but also became *too* trusting and helpful. If she kept this up, someone would hurt her sooner or later, perhaps so much so that she would never recover. In Alwera's eyes, her protégé had to be protected from herself – and it was left to her to play this role.

As she watched the food disappear down Raaka's mouth, Alwera thought hard on how to broach the topic, and when all pasties were gone, she started to speak. “You know, Raaka, I think it would be better if we left this place.” She had tried hard to keep her tone as casual as possible, so at first, her charge thought she was joking.

“Leave? Please…” Wiping away the last crumbs, Raaka looked up at Alwera’s face and only now did she realize: She hadn’t been joking at all. “What?! No way, Ellie! The people here need me! How could I just up and leave?”

“But you have to,” Alwera reminded earnestly. “While you do not want to see it for some reason, those constant spells have pushed you to your limits. Whether you want to or not, you are simply unable to help here anymore. We *have* to leave.”

“B-but!” Raaka was fumbling for words. “I can’t just abandon everyone after what I did! That the Edge attacked at all is my fault in the first place!”

“It is not!” Once again hearing how Raaka tried to take the blame for everything, Alwera’s tone became fiercer. It was just too ridiculous! “You *never* did *anything* wrong, only what you thought was best, right?”

Raaka looked down, staying silent as her friend continued. “You protected this place for so long, no one can accuse you of fleeing from any debts you may imagine. So please, Raaka,” she implored and gripped her hand. “This is the time to think of yourself. A single spell more, and you could fall asleep forever…"

"A-and what if I help without using spells? I could–"

"Raaka!" The reef-like girl flinched. "You are up against *The Edge!* Do you think you can protect this place forever!?" At that, Raaka hunched over the mattress she was sitting on. The thought of leaving all those people here behind simply didn't feel right to her. They had abandoned their homeworld, arrived on this island, and now they would be driven out once again? On top of that, there was a real chance some of them would be killed in the process, or even worse, enslaved – and at least from that fate, she had to save as many as possible. She had trained her hardest for it, and yet…

Tears gathered in Raaka's amber eyes, and Alwera's arms were around her before she knew it. "This just isn't, hick, isn't fair! Why can I still not, hick, protect anyone?"

"That is not true, Raaka." Despite the tears that fell onto her body, Alwera didn't loosen her embrace. "You did help a lot of people, did you not? I am sure you can make up for it in the future, so… ehm… there is no reason to be so sad?" Crying even harder, Raaka sobbed until her tears had run dry. When she pulled away, she looked even more exhausted than before, and for some reason, the sight of it made Alwera feel quite guilty.

"Please, do not be so glum," she said, trying to cheer her up. "Just imagine it. Once we leave, we can travel again, just like the old times! Do you not look forward to the next battlefield? I am sure there will be plenty of other people that need your help, and soon you will forget this place! Does that not sound great? How about we–"

At that point, Raaka stopped listening. It was always the same with Ellie. No matter how fierce a battle was, she could never get enough of watching it, just like the Harvest they had witnessed right before they had come to this island. While Ellie had watched on in excitement as the demonic hordes played about the fate of a whole world, Raaka had been shaken. Sure, as a Telune, she had heard stories before, how cruel the demons were and what they did to them – but she had been too young to ever witness it firsthand. And oh, just how different it had been from what she had imagined. Even now, she could remember the endless flood of demons, how they crashed into the pitiful rows of the defenders, and worse, how the noncombatants were scattered like dust between them. No matter what she tried to help, there had been little she could do but wonder: Why did the demons do all of this in the first place? Wonder and watch in horror with Ellie as the world around them slowly ended.

In the end, the only doubtful achievement she had made was to convinced Ellie to evacuate the refugees with them. However, between losing everything to the demons or losing everything by abandoning their homeworld, few people had actually taken her up on her offer. Those who did ended up penniless, and while Raaka knew that it wasn't her fault, she could very well relate to their pain. The reason she had created this camp, created Merai, had been her hope to make it up to them a little. After the powerlessness she had felt during the Harvest, it should have been the proof that she was able to help anyone at all, and yet… How did it suddenly end up like this? Although she had tried many times, she couldn't remember. Just like right now:

The night everything had started to come apart was like any other. On the same island, but in a camp much smaller than today, without vines and without protections, Raaka was sleeping peacefully in her tent until screams drove her out into the night. There she found Alwera standing in front of her own tent, looking at the sky. "W-what's going on?" she asked the flawless figure of her friend, hoping for answers, but she could only shake her blocky head.

"I am not sure, but… something is happening to the east?" Along with her reply, the screams in the distance abruptly cut off, prompting Raaka to anxiously look in their direction. What the Den was happening over there?

"I-I have a bad feeling about this," she said and suddenly ran off, but a parasol stopped her. Of course, it was Alwera's parasol, and in return for a questioning gaze, Raaka received a reprimanding reminder.

“Flying will be quicker?”

“Ah! You’re right!” After Raaka hurried onto Alwera’s back, her parasol opened above them and carried them up into the sky. Raaka’s glowing hair whipped around them while the camp zoomed out below until they could see everything: The ships that had landed on the coast, the soldiers at the fringes of the camp, and the refugees that stood in front of their burning tents watching their new homes turn to ash. It was obvious who was the cause of all this chaos, for the attackers wore a special crest. It was the Warding Shield. It was the Vanguard of World’s Edge.

“We have to get down, Ellie! Quickly!” Raaka pressured, and after the parasol shut, they plummeted downwards like falling stars, the soldiers directly beneath them. As they drew closer, a self-important voice reached their ears.

“People of the Cursed Coast! It has come to the attention of the High Citadel that you have gathered an army on this island! We mercifully condoned the presence of Otherworldlers in this remote place, but this act of aggression cannot stand unanswered! By our grace, we will now remove you from this place! Guard-Onward!”

“Guard-Onward!” the troops below replied and began to charge into the camp but were stopped by a fierce storm that suddenly howled along the coast. A few of them even went flying as every piece of burning fabric was thrust into the sea, and after the gales died along with the embers, Alwera appeared, her parasol looming high above her. Seeing the imposing sight, the soldiers hesitated for a moment, time in which a small girl detached from the intimidating figure.

"What do you mean?" Raaka questioned the captain of the assault troop, staring up at the flagship in front of her. "There're no 'acts of aggression' here. We have never done anything to anyone!" Surprised, the captain moved his gaze away from Alwera and onto the smaller figure, and as soon as he recognized what she was, a broad grin appeared on his face.

"You haven't done anything? Is that so?" The captain haughtily looked left and right, taking another look at the shore as if to prove his words. "And what is it then I am seeing before me? Upstanding Vanguards of the Edge, obstructed from their sacred duty by the very Otherworldlers I just mentioned! And what is a Telune doing here anyway?" The greed flashed up clearly in the captain's muddy eyes as he spoke the name. What a treasure he had stumbled upon on this boring mission! "Rejoice, little Telune! After we apprehend you, I promise you a more *useful* purpose than subsisting in this denhole! Don't you agree, soldiers?!"

"Yessir!"

When Raaka heard what the captain said, her heart froze over in her chest. *He was one of them*, someone else suddenly thought in her head, replacing the hope in her amber eyes with cold callousness. "I understand," the someone hissed with Raaka's mouth, her once gentle voice gruff and cold. 'Raaka only ever helped people,' that was what everyone thought, but Raaka wasn't the only one in her body. For Akara, there was only hate, for those that hunted her people, who chased after her 'hair,' and yet, the captain mistook her response for obedience. His smile turned wider, more sleazy, but only until the tides washing around the ship he stood on suddenly changed. He clearly didn't expect the flood that was now rushing up the shore, like a wave that approached land but never broke. Its dark blue swallowed the soldiers and lifted up his small fleet until a watery cliff towered over Akara's head.

"W-what are you doing!" the captain shouted down to her, angry and fearful. "Who are you to dare pick a fight with us!"

"My name doesn't matter," Akara said, a malicious grin spreading on her features. "I am only following my sacred duty – which is to remove you from this place. You know? For your act of aggression?"

Hearing his own words from earlier in reply, the captain atop the blue cliff dumbly stared down at Akara who mockingly waved a single hand. Just that small movement of hers was enough to free the masses of water she held, and suddenly, the Edge was washed away. Their ships and soldiers were pulled out onto the sea while the refugees cheered in the background, leaving only Akara's face cold as she stared after them. Unseen by anyone else, she cast a final spell so that at least the captain wouldn't return home today. He had lost his right to live the moment he looked at her with that greed in his eyes, just like everyone else who had ever revealed that sight to her. Since the day she was born, her hatred for them had not diminished, for it was endless. Just like the ocean.

Slowly, Akara lowered her hand, and her expression softened as she gave back control to a confused Raaka. Her alter ego blinked and looked around, unable to explain how the Edge had suddenly disappeared from the shore. And even today, that particular question remained a mystery.

"Raaka? Raaka, are you alright?!" A hand shook her, and when Raaka looked up, a worried Alwera was right in front of her face. Retreating a little, she quickly answered with a nod but was inwardly flustered. Why had she lost focus all of a sudden?

"Y-Yeah, I'm okay… Did you say something?"

"Yes? Are you sure you are alright?" When Raaka nodded fiercely in response, Alwera gave her a suspicious stare. Ever since they came here, she'd started to behave strangely now and then. "Anyway.

As I just said, our escape is already planned. I think we will leave around sunset."

"Leave?" Raaka echoed, just now remembering what they had been talking about before. Right, The Edge were too dangerous, and she too tired to do what was expected of her… Shaking her head, she drove away the gloomy thoughts and tried to put her mind to the future. "But how exactly are we going to leave? I am not going to harm anyone, so please don't tell me you plan on fighting your way out. This will already cause enough trouble as is."

"E-eh, *no*?" Alwera stuttered. "I would *never!*" But of course, that was a lie. She hadn't considered that in the slightest. After all, she cared not a bit about anyone here, and even the matter with Yarok had only been a substitute for what she really wanted. "And because *I knew* that you would feel that way, I even organized a little help. I–"

"*You* got help? *Reeeally*?"

At Raaka's skeptical tone, Alwera sheepishly turned away. "Yes, I did! After all, how are we supposed to get out of here without some more violent arguments? Your magic is too rough, I am not good enough at combat, and sneaking will not work this time." Raaka frowned slightly. Although Ellie was right about all of that, she still didn't want to hurt other people, especially not those she had protected for so long. Of course, her disagreement didn't go unnoticed.

"Please, Raaka, I already hired the most skillful people I could find. I am sure they can avoid hurting too many people." At least, once she had told them about that. Hopefully.

In the end, she reluctantly gave her approval. Although it was bitter for Raaka to admit, it was likely impossible to escape using purely peaceful means. Before The Edge started their attacks, she had been quite influential as far as this island was concerned, but since she slept most of the time nowadays, other powers had come to fill the void she left.

At some point in the past, the peoples of the Cursed Coast that lived around and within the towering maze had formed a loose alliance to fight against whoever hunted them. It was the leader of that alliance that had used the attacks of The Edge as a reason to take control of this island, and Raaka soon found herself a mere figurehead. Even back then when they confined her, she didn't say anything. 'It was more important to help.' That's what she thought back then, but in hindsight, maybe she should have tried to resist more fiercely.

With a bitter smile, she looked down at the main reason they couldn't use the time-tested method of 'sneaking out,' the bracelets she had received shortly after her imprisonment. Wrapped around her left arm were two silvery bands of metal that had been imbued with spells. The first one tracked her location and the other blocked access to other worlds. While Raaka did not know where the alliance got these rare artifacts, it wasn't important anymore. They kept them from fleeing alone all the same.

"Do you still remember," Alwera suddenly spoke up, "about the searching spells I asked about? I promised one to our helpers without consulting you, but that was the only way."

"Ah, yes, you did ask about that!" When Raaka's mind turned to those mysterious helpers, she suddenly turned a little more lively. "But if they agreed to come along to an Archa, does that mean we will get more companions? Who is it?! Are they nice?" With each question, she leaned in closer, while Alwera leaned farther back. What was she supposed to say here? In the first place, she hadn't asked the former Forgetful for a name, and *that demon*? Nice?! She didn't even know where to start.

"U-uhm, how about we do the introductions later? I do not want to spoil the surprise!!" With that, Alwera fled to the door and waved, but her forced smile only made Raaka more suspicious of her. "Just wait here and rest, yes? I will come pick you up when everything is ready."

The door closed for good, and Alwera disappeared, leaving Raaka sitting alone on her bed. Alwera's behavior made clear that something wasn't quite right with their new friends, but now was not the time to think about this. After all, they would be here soon.

STORYTIME

Shortly after Alwera had left, the door to Raaka's room opened another time, but it wasn't her friend who stepped through but the captain of the guards standing watch outside. He was a Canid, with a big, fluffy dog head on his shoulders, and it's expression was slightly uncomfortable as he looked left and right.

"Liam!" Raaka greeted him, trying to to sit up as soon as she noticed the guard. "Where are they?" Liam flinched, at her question or her bright, loud voice, and put one of his clawed fingers to his snout.

"Not so loud, little one. We don't want anyone to hear us, right?"

"O-Oh, yes. I'm sorry…"

"Don't be. There isn't much time." With his tongue hanging out to one side of his snout, Liam stepped out of the door, and a group of excited children stormed in to crowd tightly around Raaka's bed. But because they were what they were, they also weren't quiet at all.

"Children, pipe down!" Liam hurriedly reminded them. "Otherwise, this may be the last time you can come here. And that's not what you want, is it?" The children instantly fell silent the moment they heard his warning, while Raaka quickly turned away to hide her guilt. What Liam didn't know was that today, it didn't matter how loud or quiet the children were. This would be the last moments she would be able to share with them.

"Thank you, Liam. Really."

"It's nothing." The guard grinned broadly as he left, beginning to shut the door behind him. "This is the least I can do for saving me and those kids from the demons." With that, the door fell shut, and Liam was gone, Raaka smiling a sad smile as she stared after him. Why did the people here always have to be so friendly?

"Arwe you alwright?" said one of the children, who had climbed up onto her bed as soon as Liam left. "You look sad." Just like Liam, he also was a Canid, with ears so large they covered his eyes. At his word, Raaka strengthened her smile, completely ignoring how the dirty clothes of all the children ruined her blanket. Each and every one of them she knew by name. They were important to her.

"It's alright, Tinton," she said to the small Canid who had put his crutch over his thin legs. "You didn't visit me to talk about boring adult things, right? How have you all been doing since the last time we met?" Just like that, the children answered one after another, her own feelings all but forgotten.

"We went scavenging on the beach!" the first one replied from the crowd.

"I found a bracelet!"

"And I found a sword!"

"And I," Tinton proclaimed, "saw a demon!" At that, the other children all clicked their tongues and rolled their eyes. Raaka also wasn't amused, although for entirely different reasons.

"I told you, its dangerous for you to scavenge from the soldiers! What if you'd cut yourself on a dagger? Or something worse they carried with them? And what's that I'm hearing about a demon?" The children guiltily looked away when they saw Raaka's stern face, and a small girl oinked up to explain. Her name was Kyta and she was a cute, little Spiglet whose nose was always running. In addition, the pink dress she wore indicated that she was a bit more lucky in life than the other children. She and Tinton had always been prone to quarreling.

"Don't listen to Tinhead, sis Raaka! He simply doesn't want to admit that he slipped on the rocks." Of course, the small puppy couldn't let that accusation stand.

"No, it's true! There was an ugly, scawry monster at the beach! It's two horns werwe even longer than I am tall!"

"There was nothing there when we checked though." Hearing Kyta's condescending comment, Tinton started to growl, and Raaka intervened before they started another argument.

"Listen. It doesn't matter what you saw or found. A lot of dangerous things can be washed ashore at the beach, so promise me to not play there in the future, okay?"

"""Yes, Aunt Raaka~""" Although the children, especially Tinton, didn't really see it the same way, they reluctantly agreed.

"Good." Raaka smiled. "What story should I tell you today?" At her question, the pile of children pressed closer around her as they started to argue about a theme.

"I want to hear about knights!"

"I want to hear about princesses!"

"No, a dashing prince!"

As usual, her little rascals had to discuss a few minutes to come to a decision, but in the end, they found something they all more or less agreed on: A story about heroes. "Alright," Raaka teased, "but I'm not quite sure if you're really ready for the tale I have in mind."

"I am wready for anything!" Tinton retorted while playfully puffing out his chest. His statement, however, didn't sit quite right with one of the other children.

"You mean *we* are ready for anything! And don't be so loud, you know what Uncle Liam told us!" Kyta added, earning an annoyed stare from Tinton.

"I believe you, I believe you," Raaka interjected with a laugh that stopped their budding argument. "Then listen now as I tell you of a story as old as time. A story everyone has heard of, but few dare to speak aloud." Soon following her every word, the children were bound to Raaka's lips, painting the room in silence as they listened. "Let us remember so that we don't forget how everything began: The tale of the Everwar."

"Long ago, there was a time when there were no demons, no angels, and no wars. People were living their lives in blissful peace, staying in one world until they left it. No one had to flee, and no one had to suffer either."

Raaka paused for a moment, a moment in which the children around her all heaved wistful sighs. Oh how they wished to have lived in these times.

"But then, slowly but without warning, they started to appear: Greedy, ravenous beings that swallowed any world they appeared in. Back then, monsters were all they were called, but today, we know them under a much different name. Those monsters were the first of the demons." At her ominous tone, the children all breathed in sharply but didn't dare to interrupt.

"At first, there were just a few such cases. Not many people cared when mere rumors were all they heard of a threat that was far away, but everything changed when the Devil appeared. At his back, he led an army of demons, their twisted shapes and numbers alike darkening the earth." Raaka swallowed dryly for a moment, seeing it before her inner eye. "Led by the Devil, they swept through the worlds, their goal revenge and the greed for more. The trails of destruction they wrought, however, did not go unnoticed. Do anyone of you know what happened next?" Her gaze swept along the circle of children, finding a lifted arm at the end.

"Of course!" Kyta exclaimed, her beady eyes sparkling with excitement. "The angels!" Laughing, Raaka nodded and rewarded the little Spiglet with a pet on the head.

"That's right, Kyta. Seeing the stars in the sky erased one by one, the angels, beings of beauty and light, descended from the sky for the first time. When they saw what the demons had done to the stars, they were furious. Instantly, they rushed in to help defend the worlds besieged by the demons, and under their guidance, the remaining worlds managed to unite for the first time – together against a common foe."

Raaka paused to observe the bated breaths of all the children cuddled up around her. "But it was not enough." Gasps from everyone around her, except from Kyta, who nodded smugly at the others.

"Show-off," Tinton muttered, but fortunately, Kyta didn't hear him.

"Somehow," Raaka continued, "the demonic hordes were more numerous than the angels and all the worlds combined, and the Devil openly taunted the races with their origin. Back in the Den, he declared, the demon Queen was waiting like a kraken, giving birth to the endless hordes fueling the war, and unfortunately, time would tell that he wasn't lying. No matter how many worlds were wiped out, how many demons were killed, there were always more, and by now, all of us forgot how long the fighting went. What we still remember, however, are the titles those warmongers received. The Queen, guilty by the sea of blood her children spilled, was henceforth dyed crimson, and the Devil, too evil to be called so harmlessly, was cursed for all time as Perpetrator of All Destruction. Led by these two monsters, nothing could stop the demonic hordes from laying waste to creation, and soon, the handful of the old worlds remaining trembled before their cursed names. But then, when the signs were at their bleakest, a hero appeared."

"Yesss! Finally!" Tinton's tail wagged left and right as he put his little fists into the air.

"Stop being so loud, Tinton!" Kyta admonished. "I want to hear the story!"

"You alwready know it anyway, smarwty-pants!"

"So what?!" Kyta oinked back while Tinton growled, their foreheads almost pressed against each other. But suddenly, someone grabbed them by the scruff of their necks, pulling them over to her sides. Of course, it was Raaka.

"Don't spoil it for the others, okay? That's not fair."

"B-but–!"

"I know, Kyta. Come here now." With one hand petting Kyta's head, the other Tinton's back, Raaka continued her story. "So a hero appeared. Radiant and just and kindness incarnate he was, as if someone had read all the stories of the worlds and concentrated their goodness into a single person. In his hands, he wielded a sword that could cut anything and everything, fighting as one with a woman whose hair seemed like branches in full bloom. Together with Elysium Ysel, the leader of all angels, the hero fought against the hordes of demons until they finally faced their leader. It was a fierce battle, with many heroic sacrifices, but in the end, the Perpetrator of All Destruction was finally defeated. Cut by the hero's sword and drenched in the light of the Elysium, he dissolved without a single trace. The rest of the demons, without a warrior to lead them, were driven out of the worlds, and thus creation was saved. Since that day, remember that children, we all owe the angels, and the hero, our eternal thanks."

"""Yes, Aunt Raaka!""" her rascals' bright voices answered, pressing tightly together on the mattress. After the happy end of the gloomy story, their smiles appeared even more radiant than usual.

"The hewro is so cool!" Tinton exclaimed in excitement, his tail wagging against Raaka's side as she petted his head. "Can't you tell us morwe about him?"

"But, sis Raaka," Kyta interrupted Tinton as if it was the most natural thing to do. "If the Perpetrator had been defeated back then, what happened to the Crimson Queen?"

"Oh, that…" Raaka awkwardly scratched her head. "I'm afraid this is the only story I know about her, although I always imagine that she's been leading the demons ever since. But who can really say for sure?" Kyta, clearly dissatisfied by that answer, wanted to retort when two long and two short knocks suddenly sounded from the entrance. After it opened, Liam's head stuck inside.

"Are you done? Part of the shift is changing soon."

With a hesitant nod, Raaka turned to smile at the children, giving Kyta and Tinton one last hug. "Alright, all of you. Don't do anything stupid until we meet again. Understood?"

"I would neverw!" Tinton replied while Kyta rolled her eyes behind him.

"Don't worry, sis Raaka. I will do my best to watch out for this numbskull." Just like that, Raaka saw them leave, her bed emptying one by one as she kept the same mask of a smile on her face. The children were just about to vanish for good when Tinton, supported by Kyta because of his crutch, turned around to smile at her.

"But next time! Next time you will tell us morwe about the hewro… Wright?"

Seeing the look in his eyes, she had no choice but to agree. "Y-yes, Tinton. Look out for the others too, okay?" He nodded, hobbling past Liam and out of sight. With the children gone, the guard, still gripping the door's handle, gave her a short bow. Short, but not disrespectful.

"Thank you for always educating them a bit."

"Oh, those are just stories," she replied lightly, her voice constricting just a little. "They aren't that educating."

But Liam barked a deep laugh before shaking his head. "Anything that keeps them off the streets. See you tomorrow." Nodding weakly, Raaka tried to remember his big, fluffy face as best as she could before the door closed, but it did so all too quickly. It had been so nice to see them… one last time.

As the tears started to stream down her face, she leaned back, muffling her cries in her pillow so Liam wouldn't hear. It hurt her so much to leave them behind. And she hated it.

ESCAPE VESSEL

Her talk with Raaka done, Alwera left the military district, put on her Minotaur disguise, and approached the western edge of the city. Like everywhere on its borders, the green wall of vines towered above the tents around her, but some space had been freed so that people could pass through.

It was one of those exits that Alwera now left from, and on the other side, countless vines branching off from the wall came into view. Placed on top of each of them were warehouses and wooden piers, and by reaching up and down and far into the blue water, the gigantic plant helped to form the makeshift and confusing harbor of this city.

In the mornings and evenings, this area would be teeming with small boats used for fishing, but with them out on the sea, only a handful of bigger ships were left towering between the vines. Although most of them were owned by the kind of merchants greedy enough to ignore the threat of the Edge, Alwera didn't particularly mind how they profited from the people. There was much worse inside this harbor – like the ship she was just passing by. It was a galley, with many rows sticking out into the air, and on the side of its hull hung a sign that openly advertised its business. It said, "Happy Harriet's Helpful Human

Resources – Special offer, only today! We're now buying three people for the price of four!" Reading the provocative message, Alwera shook her head and walked away. That those slavers dared to return at all after what happened last time Raaka saw one of them was… not quite surprising. After all, Happy Harriet's was the most risk-loving company she knew.

As the slave galley fell away for good, Alwera came up to the reason she had come here, the ship she planned to use for their escape. Just recently arrived, it was matured and old with weathered masts holding triangular as well as square sails. Its hull, too, showed its turbulent history, left a colorful patchwork of wood created by countless repairs. Even now, Alwera could hear construction noises from inside, likely from a recent battle. All in all, the sight of the ship ahead of her, *The Patchy*, didn't necessarily inspire confidence. And yet, they had little choice.

Walking up the plank and onto the ship, Alwera was planning to search for the captain when the constant hammering from below suddenly stopped. There was a loud bang and a string of curses before an even louder door slammed open, and a squat, grumpy man came into view. His sagging, gray-pink face held a round, drooping nose in front of a lipless mouth and two black slits for eyes that seemed to glare at everything. Those features, arranged as if to represent the immensity of his bad mood, were completed by a flat cap with fleshy spikes of hair peeking out from below it.

As the man hobbled out of the ship, his nose held a contest with his hair to see who jiggled the most, but it was the huge wrench visible behind his shoulder who beat them all, followed closely by the tools dangling from his belt. This person seemed to be a mechanic – and an angry one at that. "Ugh, whatcha want, scum?" he barked at Alwera with a voice as annoyed as his looks. "We ain't buyin' nothin' so piss off!" Alwera, however, showed no signs of leaving even after hearing this joke of a greeting. They really, really needed this ship.

Seeing that the Minotaur didn't leave, the mechanic put one hand to his wrench and pulled down his flat cap with the other. To him, this looked like another case of 'idiot on top of his ship,' and his face jiggled like jelly as he threatened closer to fix it. Seeing his anger, Alwera hurried to defuse the situation.

"Please excuse my intrusion, sir, but I wish to hire this ship. Please, may I speak to the captain?" It was a critical blow. Hearing the revolting politeness from one of those Minotaur savages, the mechanic stumbled over his legs and barely managed to use his wrench to support himself. But although Alwera had been so diplomatic, his reply remained terribly rude.

"So what?! And I wanna swim inna tub full of gold, but cha got one? What a surprise, ya don't! Don't make me repeat this, ya dumb cow!" His wrench already lifted, the mechanic was about to come within hitting range when another voice, old and shrill, pierced through the planks of the ship.

"Boblob! Stop harassing our customers! How often do I have to tell you!?" The surly mechanic froze instantly before slowly, very slowly, turning his head with a creak to stare through the wood and down at the voice. The glimpse of his face Alwera got when he glanced back at her was even more annoyed than annoyance itself, and naturally, his voice was the same.

"That fucking tin can!" Boblob, not trying to lead Alwera at all, stormed back through the door he came through and into the dim deck waiting below. She hurriedly followed, squeezing her Minotaur body into the ship and down the narrow, steep stairs leading inside. At their end waited an open door, and without a trace of Boblob, Alwera hesitantly stepped through.

On the other side of the elaborate frame, she found a room quite big for a ship, with large stained-glass windows at the back that flooded her sight with light. As she was blinded, a high, squeaky voice spoke from somewhere. "There they are! See?! Our disguised friend has arrived!?"

Flinching at the meaning of the words, Alwera tried to recognize who was speaking until the brightness faded and a hefty office table appeared from within. Decorated with golden bands of metal, its reddish-brown surface was empty except for a single decanter containing thick crimson liquid – or at least it appeared that way before a small, crab-like machine jumped out behind it, the likes of which Alwera had never seen before.

“See?!” The crab turned around to the windows, the two googly eyes stuck to its front bobbing around as it moved. Its body was metal covered in runes, and a ruby gem could be seen floating beneath layers of moving clockwork. “See!” the crab repeated more forcefully, but the dim chair standing in front of the bright windows remained silent. Not like that kept it from continuing. “I told ya, Blobby was just about to kick them out! He’s so dull!”

Across the desk and in a high wingback chair sat an elderly woman. The impression she gave reminded of a kind grandma relaxing from a fulfilled life, but the eyepatch and tricorn she wore didn’t quite fit. She seemed so old, her hair that framed her wrinkles was a pure, frosty white, and as it fell down in a loose braid holding a silver hook at its end, its colorless color clashed beautifully with the vibrant red velvet of the seat behind her.

Rather than answering any of the machine’s questions, the woman silently returned its wobbly gaze, and yet, it continued to speak, the burden of listening to its nonsense leaving her a little older with every word. “I mean, there has to be something wrong with his head, right? I’ll never understand how he could create this magnificent me! You, too, think it’s a fluke, right? Right?!”

Refusing to answer, the old woman lifted a hand and brought up the pipe she held to her mouth. It was a Teapipe, a long straw attached to a cup and a saucer, and the liquid inside bubbled softy as she pulled in fresh air. Steam sprang forth from inside, and milky ribbons spread all the way to the door, leaving a rusty aroma in their wake. Of course, Alwera, a Papersnip, couldn't smell it. She was still standing there, slightly confused.

Why did the woman still refuse to reply, and why did that Construct continue to talk although it was obviously ignored? It spoke so much there was not a single pause for her to introduce herself, and so, she simply watched on. "And do you know the worst?" More monologue from the Construct. "Sometimes, when Blobby sleeps, his nose falls into his mouth, and then he starts licking it! I don't really understand, I don't know noses, but isn't that disgusting?"

Together with that last insult, Alwera was suddenly pushed aside, and Boblob stormed past her and into the room. A strange fishing net in both hands, he homed in on the machine on the table. He had obviously heard every one of the insults it had spoken.

"You heap of scrap metal! Ya really went too far this time! Come 'ere, I'll teach your manners!" With that, the net went flying over the table, but the crab simply scuttled aside and let the woman get caught in its stead. At full speed, the net hit her square in the face, spilling a bit of tea from her pipe.

"Boblob!" she yelled angrily. "How dare ya waste my precious drugs!" The net around her was quickly ripped off, but by the time she had freed herself, Boblob was already lunging towards her – or rather, the crab-like machine sitting on her desk.

"Ahh!" With a squeak and a jump, the crab evaded once more and clung to the ceiling where it spoke a last blow down to its creator. "Ha! Update score: Blobby 6, Shiny 552 – Done. Commence command: Flee!" And flee it did, moving sideways towards Alwera and passing just inches from her head. Their gazes met in the doorframe, and for a moment, she saw its googly eyes rolling left and right, more ridiculous than they had any right to be.

While the Construct disappeared into the rest of the ship, uncaring of the chaos it left in its wake, Boblob was still sailing through the air directly at the woman in her chair. To anyone with common sense, the result was already clear, but the elderly woman did not try to escape the living cannonball hurtling at her. After putting out a hand, she caught Boblob's chin like one would a ball, and the sound of crunching bone swept quietly through the room.

"Are ya *so* intent on annoying me, Boblob?! After what happened just recently!?" There were a few more little crunches, but while the woman wasn't worried, Boblob blinked furiously. His face was so squeezed up that he couldn't answer, so the woman simply continued. "Ugh, of course you wouldn't say anything. Out of my sight and back to ya repairs or something! Give me a break!"

With that, he was unceremoniously thrown out of the room, directly at Alwera who barely had the wits to dodge in time. Pressed against the wall outside of the door, Boblob raced past her eyes before disappearing in the darkness behind the stairs. "And Boblob!" the woman yelled after him. "Dontcha dare ask for another raise until ya finally fix that sullen mug of yours!"

A loud crash could be heard, and silence befell the ship. Slowly, very slowly, Minotaur Alwera, who was still hiding behind the door, peeked around its frame and into the cabin. The elderly but obviously quite active woman was now relaxing in her chair, doing nothing but watch the steam gather below the ceiling. Somehow, the long draws she took from her pipe suddenly seemed very peaceful. Looking at this motley crew, maybe it was for the best that she hadn't been forced to ask them for even more help.

Still unsure, Alwera carefully stepped inside the cabin. "I extend my greetings," she said and bowed, her deep Minotaur voice jarringly loud after the quaint silence. "Are you the captain of this ship?"

Hearing her, the woman in the chair lowered her gaze, blowing out some steam through her nose. "Yes, that would be me," she replied, and showed a crooked smile that let more steam waft to her laughing eyes. "Karoly's the name, but what do *I* owe the honor of your mysterious visit?" Each word was followed by more steam escaping her mouth, and Alwera sheepishly scratched her head as she realized once more that her disguise had already been revealed.

"I came here to hire you for passage to Empyrea, or, more specifically, to Alhena Tesera."

"Ah," Karoly sat up, "the local Archa, yes? You *did* come to the right place, but, dontcha take this the wrong way, only if ya have the money. And you don't really look like it." Hearing her blunt remark, Alwera noticed that the captain wasn't entirely wrong. For certain reasons, she did indeed carry little money with her – and what little she had was definitely not enough to hire a ship. Actually, Raaka could had given her more, but she forgot to ask her when she suddenly had to flee from the questions about their new companions…

Sighing, Alwera hid one hand behind her back as she resolved herself to use her emergency fund. She really was reluctant to waste it on something mundane like this. Where Karoly couldn't see, a part of her disguise quickly reverted back into paper, and from it appeared a slim wooden case. Holding it almost reverently with both hands, Alwera lumbered forward to carefully place it on the captain's desk. "Maybe this will change your mind," she said to her and stepped back, watching while Karoly opened it.

Lifting one brow, the captain slid away the lid, revealing a single cube of glass resting on a small cushion. Between its corners sat a violet gem, a splinter so small it was almost hard to see. Despite that, everyone who saw it couldn't help but be captivated, gazes sucked into a place deeper than the deepest sea. Some, they rumored, had even drowned inside of it.

At the sight of the gem, one of the rarest objects in all creation, Karoly was shocked. "A freakin' Dreamshard!" she shouted in excitement, and even lifted her eyepatch slightly to make sure – but this gem was the real deal. "This is–" the captain suddenly stopped and smoothed her expression, "…*barely* enough."

"I would sure hope so," Alwera replied as dryly as Karoly's earlier shock was real, along with a faint trace of bitterness. A Dreamshard was worth way more than a simple passage on any ship, but they were short on time as it was. After informing the captain about the particulars of their deal, Karoly eventually added a condition of her own.

"Nothing of this should be a problem." The case with her payment was stored in a drawer of her desk. "But our last job did cost us a few of ma crew, so… if there's any trouble, everyone on board's to help. You don't mind, do ya?" Thinking nothing about it, Alwera agreed with a nod, and Karoly stood up with a broad but slightly melancholic smile – although that may have just been her imagination.

"BOBLOB!" Karoly shouted into the rest of the ship, "SEND THE ROOKIES TO GATHER EVERYONE! WE'RE BACK ON CONTRACT!" As expected of a captain, her voice was loud enough to make Alwera understand what it meant to have hurting ears although she didn't have any. While she was still holding her head, the captain now turned back to her: "CAPTAIN KAROLY, AT YOUR SERVICE!"

Seeing her hand extended over the desk, Alwera, still a little dazed, gripped it to seal their deal. While her huge Minotaur hand seemed much sturdier than Karoly's daintier one, the grip of the captain was so strong that it nearly crumpled her paper body. When Alwera tried to wrench her hand away, Karoly let go and picked up a rapier leaning behind the desk. It was a thin sword with a handguard shaped like a teakettle, and the unusual style easily captivated Alwera. The whole time the captain saw her off the ship, using the sword as a cane, Alwera's eyes remained fixed on the beautiful blade. Before she knew it, she was standing alone on the pier, Karoly's sword nowhere in sight.

A little disappointed, Alwera turned around to leave when the door to *The Patchy* flew open once again. It seemed some of the crew had come out.

"Don't fuck this up, kids, or we'll leave ya here to rot!" It was Boblob, and fluttering in front of him…

"A-ayee, ayee, Boblob! I swear wee won't betray your trust, geeezer!"

"Right, t-there's no reason to hurt us again, gramps... right, Shanty?!

"Whaddya mean, *geezer! Gramps?!* Just wait till I get ma hands on ya dipshits!

"I-Iahahahaha!"
"Iahahahaaaa!"

Shanty and Shanza, the siblings widely known as the curse of this city, seemed to be the rookies Karoly had ordered around earlier. Alwera felt her legs buckle. Why?! Why had the captain done this? On a ship, there would be no way to avoid them forever!

While Alwera knelt on the pier in front of *The Patchy*, her soul leaving her slowly, Shanty and Shanza hastily beat their wings to escape from the fuming Boblob. Of course, they paid no attention to the disguised Alwera as they shot along the warehouses, and they didn't care either how she lifted her head to look after them. Although there were few people around, the annoying siblings managed to bump into everyone they came across, and it almost looked intentional – because it was. Alwera's head dropped back down. This trip would surely be worse than any of her nightmares.

A few minutes passed before Alwera managed to stand up, slowly stumbling back towards the military district. She really wanted to take a break now, so much so that she didn't pay attention to the way ahead. And promptly, she got the result: Someone bumped into her, shoving her aside with rough movements.

“Out of the way!”

After barely holding onto a warehouse right above the frothing waves, Alwera turned to yell at whoever was so incredibly rude but quickly stopped. It hadn’t been a single person but a large group of carriers, and considering all the guards that surrounded the bulky crate they heaved around, their load must have been quite important. A string of smaller chests followed the first one, and Alwera watched them pass by until a Dzorok came up at the end of the train.

Dzorok was what they called Yarok’s people. This one was a few heads smaller than their leader and wore lighter armor that only protected his vitals. Without metal casing, Dzorok looked a lot like humans but larger and thicker and with bony plates instead of skin which formed a crown around their heads, and not to forget the three legs, two in the front, and one in the back, and – okay, they were nothing like humans, but that wasn’t really the point here. In the end, the important part was that all Dzorok in this place were commanded by Yarok – and this made Alwera wonder what was inside the crates for one of theirs to be guarding them.

Following her curiosity and partly because she needed a distraction, Alwera hid behind the closest warehouse to observe the mysterious procession. She didn’t have to wait long until they reached their destination. Surprisingly, it was the slave galley she had seen earlier.

This was a first. The alliance the Dzorok were part of didn't work with slavers, and something that needed such a large crate, what could it be… Armor?! Weapons!? Suddenly shaking off her bad mood, Alwera almost performed a small dance. Because of their escape, she had already given up on the reward Yarok promised for her 'work,' but this was a good opportunity to get what she was owed.

Humming a happy tune, Alwera gripped the skin on her Minotaur arm and plucked out a strip of paper, but when she threw it up into the air, it didn't fall towards the ground. Instead, the white square soared up from the tangled piers and into the sky where it folded into the pale copy of a seagull. Except for the other seagulls around it, no one noticed how the fake bird flew down to the slave ship, landing soundlessly in an open porthole where it looked over all of the dim cargo hold. Back at the warehouse, an expectant smile spread across Alwera's face as she imagined what she would get to see there. Weapons! Armor! Wait for me~!

THINGS SET IN MOTION

A groaning sound escaped the mouth of the demon but instantly suffocated in the darkness surrounding him. Just a moment ago, he had been walking through the city, trying to find his way back, so how did he suddenly end up on the ground? Dazed, he sat up, but the movement only made him notice the pain in his heart, scorching like a pulsing sea of flames. It was the truest form of his hunger, telling him that plenty of time must have passed since his last meal, but its burning waves had grown so strong already that he couldn't even focus on taking out the souls he had found. Instead, he laid gasping on the floor like a fish on land, glimpses of the planks around him appearing in the minuscule breaks. Where was he? What had happened? Although those were vital questions, he was in too much pain to find any answers, until the fire suddenly diminished from one moment to the next. But this silence was just the calm before the storm. Breathing heavily, the demon craned his neck as a shadow fell over his head, for over his inner eye was now towering the final wave of agony. It was so much stronger and higher than any before, there was no way that he could endure it. "I'm sorry, everyone," the demon whispered, his thinning vision falling to the floor – until it suddenly stopped at a small girl standing in the way of the gathering wave. Like a single soldier facing an army, her ocean back was turned towards him, the cascades of her glowing hair so long that they barely stopped at the ground. Suddenly, the girl spoke, still staring at the pain towering above them.

The throne of water needs an heir. Serve, and you will be saved.

Her voice sounded firm and resolute, but the demon was too weak to understand anything but the warmth they carried. Or was it just the pain that had begun to crash down around them? "Please," he breathed to the girl as the world was swallowed by red. "Please help me." Together with his words, the ground toppled over, and a small light shattered on the back of his neck, not that he noticed any of it. From now on, the pain would be in control, and it had but a single goal in mind: Ending its own hunger.

If that is your wish.

The girl's voice belatedly swept through the red.

Inside of Happy Harriet's slave galley, a tremor went through the floor of the cargo hold as the side of a bulky crate crashed into its planks. With a bang, the lid of the container came off, and its contents tumbled precisely into a circle of square symbols.

Finally freed, the demon jumped onto all fours, its tail snapping left and right like that of an angry tiger.

Outside of the strange formation and next to the now empty crate stood two soldiers, and the feral demon instantly jumped at them with a hiss. Clearly, its target was their juicy souls, but the claws swinging through the air never reached them. Right as the soldiers were about to die, an invisible wall flashed up and repelled the demon so violently that it spun around like a broken doll, but it didn't learn, as though his former intelligence had been a lie all along. Again and again, the same attempt led to the same result until the soldiers outside started to laugh.

"Ha, look at that thing. That's a demon? More like a mindless beast." The soldier's words dripped with ridicule, and his companion agreed with a doubtful expression.

"You're right, but do you really think this thing can buy us some time? I'm sure the Edgies will off this animal in a flash once we deliver it."

"Why do you care? Orders are orders. Make sure you don't drink too much again. If you're not sobered up by tonight and get your punishment, don't come complain to me like last time."

With the demon secured inside the circle, the joking soldiers disappeared between the rest of the cargo and missed something vital in the process. Right below the ceiling, in an open porthole, sat a stunned paper bird. And it had watched everything.

The end of the day was drawing closer over the square covered island when the flaps of the traveler's tent suddenly burst open and a huge Minotaur stomped inside. The traveler was currently lazing on his bed but looked up at the noise and frowned when he saw Alwera's broad grin.

"Hellooo, Mr. Forgetful~" The glee and mockery were thick in her voice. "Guess what I found when I was at the harbor? A *miserable demon* trapped in a ship! Can you not even take care of your pets? Who knew a Godly could be *this* pitiful."

Hearing about his newest acquisition, which was still missing, the traveler jumped up from his bed. "What do you mean, trapped in a ship? Explain yourself!" And Alwera gladly did, with as much happiness as she could muster. Halfway through, the traveler started to hold his head, and when she ended, he had to sit back down for a moment. "Oh, I don't believe this. I thought I picked up a demon, so why did he suddenly become a princess? Isn't saving one of them enough already?"

Alwera laughed but only until the traveler stood up and tried to storm out of the tent. "What are you doing?" Her tone was genuinely confused.

"Oh, you see, I have to save my princess, don't I?"

"*What?!* You are joking, right? What nonsense are you talking about in the first place? It is no princess but a *demon* that you want to save!" Alwera couldn't understand, while the traveler couldn't understand why she couldn't.

"I still have to save him? After all, I can't leave one of my actors behind if they haven't been worked sufficiently. Don't you agree that would be terribly inefficient?"

"No! Wait, yes I do, but– ugh! This is why you are so annoying!" She had been in such a good mood after observing the cargo hold, the idea that her harmless tease would lead to this kind of disaster hadn't even occurred to Alwera. She really had thought they would leave without the demon, but only to ended up triggering his rescue. What a disaster!

Taking Alwera's dejected silence for agreement, the traveler tried to walk past her a second time, but a second time, she got in his way. This slowly stopped being funny. At the traveler's glare, Alwera took a step back and quickly explained. Maybe she could still make up for her mistake. "I-It is alright, you can rescue your 'princess' or whatnot, but we have to free Raaka before that. Otherwise, there will be soldiers everywhere! And incidentally, you are not allowed to kill any of them!"

"I see." The traveler calmed down a little. "I get the first part, but why no killing?"

"Because Raaka is a caring person! Littering the floor with bodies in her wake will definitely make her furious." But Alwera's words didn't really convince, and so, the traveler started walking again. "On top of that!" she added hastily. "If you really want Raaka to sneak into an Archa, which I still think won't ever work by the way, angering her is the last thing you need, right?"

The traveler stopped in his tracks. More or less, that had been the plan, so she *did* have a point there. "Ugh, alright, alright, no killing. But then, how are we going to reach her without attracting attention?"

Alwera grinned, and her Minotaur face broke out into a nasty smile. "It gladdens me that you asked." The traveler suddenly had a bad feeling about this. "Let me introduce you to the disguise you didn't know you needed."

Between the traveler's tent and the military district, Alwera was moving through the streets completely undisguised. In her arms, she held a struggling bundle of fur, a small kitten that was as adorable as it was pettable. "Stop fidgeting!" she whispered admonishingly. "This is hard enough already!" As if listening to her commands, the kitten went from struggling to mewling until they reached the gate to the closed-off district.

This time, too, none of the guards stopped Alwera from entering, but because her unapproachable character didn't fit with the small cat, they got plenty of strange looks. If anyone wondered, however, she could just say that it was a pet to cheer up Raaka. And in the first place, who would be suspicious of a cat? Everyone liked them, right?

"Y-you! What are you planning to do with that *thing!?*"

It seemed that one of the soldiers in front of their barrack, the guard captain at that, was quite repulsed by the sight of the kitten. Maybe he had suffered severe trauma involving cuteness, or maybe it was because he was similar to a bipedal dog. Alwera wasn't sure, but regardless, her perfect disguise had failed.

"It's just to cheer up our savior," she answered with a cramped smile, and after an uncertain pause, the guard reluctantly let her pass. Alwera sighed as she walked through the short hallway and stopped in front of Raaka's room. Next time she needed a disguise, maybe she should try a lizard instead of a cat.

Still thinking about that, Alwera opened the door and found Raaka awake and ready. She was sitting on her bed, her shoulders and chest now covered by a plain shawl held by a clamshell brooch, and similar trinkets had been added to her short pants. Together with the gray-blue tone of the fabric that matched Raaka's ocean skin, her outfit clearly showed her closeness to the sea – although the tiny leather bag slung over her shoulder was somewhat of an exception.

That Raaka was awake at all, however, was a bit of a surprise to Alwera. She had expected her protégé to be fast asleep, but there she was, the bags below her eyes even deeper. Alwera simply didn't know that after the children had left, Raaka had been too busy crying to think of sleep, so she was quite relieved when Alwera finally entered her room. Relieved, and instantly distracted by the adorable being she saw hanging in the arms of her friend.

"Ahh! A cat! A cat! Give it to me! Let me pet it!" The kitten had vanished from Alwera's arms before she could react, and Raaka spun wildly around the room as she rubbed the 'kitten' against her cheek with her eyes closed in happiness. This way, she didn't notice that the cat was quite strange. Although Raaka clearly held it in her little arms, something invisible around it seemed to stop her embrace from reaching it completely. Seeing this, Alwera finally awoke from her stupor.

"Ah, Raaka! Put down that cat! Quickly!" The words had barely left her mouth when her spells broke, and the kitten suddenly became an adult man. Now much heavier than a moment before, the stranger went flying from Raaka's little arms and right into the closest wall, and with the weight in her arms gone, Raaka instantly opened her eyes. "W-what?" she asked tearfully. "Where's the kitten?" As if to answer her question, the stranger slowly slid down the wall until his head hit the floor with a dull thud. Startled, Raaka hurried toward the odd Cat-man, trying to make sure he wasn't hurt. Extending a hand to check on his breathing, just in that moment, the traveler's eyes shot open. And of course, he did the only thing appropriate when he saw the hand closing in on his face: He bit down on Raaka's four webbed fingers like the cat he played.

"Argh! What the dent?!"

"Meow~!"

Raaka hurriedly backed off, holding her aching hand, while the traveler tried to pose like a kitten. But after a moment of silence, he couldn't keep up the act any longer. He started to retch. "Did you know that you taste fishy?" Raaka's face started to twitch.

"I dare you to call me fishy again! Going around and *biting* people? Who are you, and what are you doing in my room?!" Being attacked on first sight, even Raaka's friendliness had soured to anger. It was a situation that could easily escalate, so Alwera quickly intervened.

"It is alright, Raaka, this is the help I was talking about. We really have to hurry, so are you–"

"Yes! This is the handy help speaking!" The traveler pushed her aside while righting his hat and wiping his mouth. "Pleased to make your acquaintance, little Witch. I sure hope you can help me too." But Raaka's hairless brows remained furrowed as she looked uncertainly at the odd stranger towering above her.

"Help you? Maybe if you stop biting people!" The traveler quickly opened his mouth to retort, but was stopped by another voice.

"All of this can wait!" Alwera reminded them, some trace of desperation in her voice. "Instead of discussing payment, how about we try to escape first? Come, Raaka, give me your arm." As Raaka was pulled over to Alwera, she shot a last resentful look at the traveler who shrugged in response. Alwera wasn't wrong: At the moment, it was more important to rescue the demon and escape, although…

"In that case, Lady Paper, you too should save staring at the Witch for later." Alwera, though, ignored him as she knelt and pulled down one of the silver bracelets clasped around Raaka's arm. "If I do not remove this before we leave, the guards will be able to follow our every step. Well, on the other hand, they will also be alerted once it is gone. So stay quiet now, and get ready to leave."

With that, Alwera fell silent, and she began to stroke softly along the silver of the first bracelet. Where her finger passed, bands of northern lights wormed up from the shiny silver and out into the air, threads of carpets woven into bigger carpets. Their coils were the essence of the bracelet's spell, and with each shift of their colors and each twist of their strings, the meaning of the whole could change completely. It was common knowledge among the mages that even the simplest spell, once cast, was impossible to understand, and yet, Alwera seemed to know what she was doing. With patient experience, she studied the weave in front of her, and only with certainty did her eyes close and her work begin: The glowing ball of threads found themselves between her arms, quivering expectantly under her hands that stroked along their tips like a pianist playing their instrument. Her fingers pressed a sparkling strand, pulled another, and inky blackness spilled forth, strange, square symbols that moved deeply into the glowing fabric.

Curious about Alwera's mysterious magic, the traveler peeked over her shoulder. Threads were pulled, cut and tightened, rearranging the spell until it petrified, black cloth crumbling to white. The meaning of all of this evaded him, but he at least recognized what it was Alwera was using there. Black Magic, The Great Work, Abjuration, even to him, an obscure and ancient technique. While he couldn't use it himself, he still remembered the explanation he got from the only other practitioner he had ever met: Magic to dissolve other magic.

Watching for several interesting minutes, the traveler waited until all of the spell had vanished from under Alwera's hands. There was a soft click, and the bracelet clattered to the floor, dull and lifeless. "They will be here soon," Alwera declared as she opened her eyes, walking to the far side of the room after standing up. A window, although small, was hanging right above her. "This is the fastest way out," she said, and Raaka instantly followed her – but the traveler was doubtful. The window Alwera had pointed to was way smaller than he had imagined. He wasn't even sure he could fit through!

"Do I look like I have time for a diet, Lady Paper?! Step aside!" Accompanying the traveler's words, a thin, quill shaped sword appeared in his hand, its pommel shaped like the nib of a fountain pen. Alwera barely had the time to evade the silvery swings running through the air, cutting an oddly hand-shaped hole into the wooden wall. The empty street outside as background, the traveler spun around, presenting his work with a flourish that dispelled his blade. While Raaka was too busy sulking, Alwera had to suppress a chuckle at the somewhat special shape of this new exit. The traveler, nodding in approval, was the first to leave. "Everyone! Let's go save princess number two!" Out into the open he stepped, full of excitement, but had to stop after a single step. "Ah!" His gaze slowly turned back at Alwera. "Where is it we are going?"

Adding another sigh to an increasingly long list, Alwera rolled her flat eyes as she pushed him aside to take the lead. Obviously, the next stop would be their escape ship lying in wait at the harbor – and they had to hurry before too much trouble could come their way.

Their group quickly left the now broken room just in time for the guards to appear shortly after. But all they found was no trace of the Witch – except a hole in the wall clearly left to mock them with its special shape: A hand giving the middle finger.

"DAMN IT!" the dog-headed guard captain, Liam, growled, almost dying of anger as soldiers piled up behind him. "R-Raaka! S-She's gone! The Edge?! Notify Yarok and gather everyone else! WE HAVE TO SAVE HER!" His subordinates dispersed at once, and Liam was left alone in the empty room, visibly distraught. "Mom really was right," he muttered as he rubbed his eyes and left. "Cats are a bad omen…"

Leaving their barrack behind, Alwera ushered them through the military district, sticking to the emptiest alleys while the traveler and Raaka followed her. By now, the guards had certainly found out about their escape, and yet, it was strangely silent. No soldiers were patrolling, and it felt like the whole area had been deserted quite some time ago.

Despite the apparent safety, Raaka's head kept anxiously swiveling around, and so she quickly found the strange statues standing here and hanging there. It had been quite some time since she had last walked through the city this way, and they were the only unfamiliar sight to her. "What are those?" she asked Alwera, her gaze staying fixed on an especially large statue that was already disappearing behind them. Her friend, however, was reluctant to answer – and so the traveler replied in her stead.

"Aren't they funny? I know they don't look that way at all, but apparently, they are supposed to be you."

"Me?" Raaka wondered, scrutinizing the next statue even more thoroughly. Maybe if she wore a mop on her head, they would resemble her a little – but unfortunately, she didn't, and that wasn't the case. Some people would have definitely been insulted by this, but these doubtful compliments were not what bothered her. "Why would anyone put up statues of me?"

The traveler, despite Alwera's desperate attempts to signal him to shut his mouth, just didn't get it. "You should be proud! I heard it's because people were so thankful for everything you did for them." Coughing violently, Raaka nearly stumbled over her own feet. The people she was going to abandon had put up statues of her!? Throwing an accusing look at Alwera, her friend simply mouthed a 'later' in response – but this did nothing to lift the weight on Raaka's conscience. A bit more uncertain than before, she walked at the back of their short train, missing how the traveler received a paper elbow into his side. "Ouch! What was that for?" Alwera, however, was too annoyed to answer.

A few streets later, she signaled their group to stop. Around the corner lay the wall that divided the military district from the rest of the city, and now they understood why no one had bothered to search for them. The only gate leading outside was tightly closed, a ton of guards clotting the streets and a handful of scouts flying in the skies. No matter how they tried to approach, someone would spot them instantly. “Well, that was fast,” Alwera said dryly as she turned towards the traveler. “Go, hired hand. Get rid of them.” Ignoring her haughty order, the traveler, too, peeked around the wall. There *really* were a lot of guards. He didn’t want to.

“Why do we need to go through the gate? Can’t we just cross the wall somewhere else?” But Alwera simply laughed quietly at his naive ideas.

“Just because you can cut through our flimsy barrack, it does not mean that the wall of the camp is the same. The bricks are solid, enchanted stone, controlled by regular air patrols. Not to mention staying undiscovered, it is simply impossible to get through.”

“Oh, Lady Paper, you have to believe.” The traveler shook his head in disappointment. “Otherwise, your dreams will never come true.”

“Argh! You simply do not want to work! We do not have time for your silly games!”

“What did you say!?” the traveler asked back, putting his hands over his ears. “I can’t hear you!” He walked away from the gate, and Alwera and Raaka had no choice but to follow – not that Alwera wasn’t angry. The whole time, from the gate up to the closest dead end bordering the wall, she complained, and even there she only fell silent because of the scouts passing overhead.

"Why do you have to waste our time like this?" she asked once more when the coast was clear, but the traveler simply hurried up to that 'solid, enchanted stone' she was so certain of. Summoning his Fountain Blade, there was a cut, and the stone bricks simply clattered onto the ground. At the hand shaped hole now gaping in the wall, Alwera thought she could understand a little of what the guards would feel once they faced it.

"Wha-wha–! How did you–?"

"Believe, Lady Paper, believe."

It was incredibly frustrating. The traveler's smug grin, so unreasonable and unpredictable, were part of the reason she hated beings like him. While the Forgetful made it look so simple, Alwera herself would have never managed to overcome this wall. Not to mention destroying the bricks, even flying above it would have been impossible with the flat buildings providing ample vision to the scouts passing by. Really, until now, their escape had been far too easy.

"HEY, YOU!" a rough voice suddenly called out behind them. "What are you doing to that wall?! Stop right there!" Now standing in the entrance of the not-so-dead end were a couple of guards. "GET THEM!" they shouted while Alwera cursed under her breath. This jinx was definitely on her.

"TIME TO RUN, PEOPLE!" The traveler dashed off, forgetting that he wasn't the only one who had to escape. Behind him, Alwera stayed last and covered for Raaka, who struggled like a child being chased around by adults. Her legs simply were too short, and Alwera could only try to spur on her exhausted protégé. Unfortunately, with the nonexistent strength of a Papersnip, they would only fall back further even if she carried her.

"How about you help us out?!" Alwera eventually called out to the traveler running in front of them. They were so close to the harbor now, even a blind chicken could find the way, so he had used this opportunity to rush a good distance ahead. According to their contract, he had to save his demon, and time was of the essence. But Alwera's call reminded him that he wasn't alone anymore.

Taking a look over his shoulder, the traveler flinched, realizing that without the Witch this whole endeavor would have been pointless. He couldn't give the guards a chance to get even closer. With a rustling sound like birds taking flight, his body burst into a cloud of feathers and reappeared behind the Witch, swiping her off the street like a thief would a pocket.

"What was that?!" Alwera shrieked, Raaka's head bobbing up and down as they increased their pace, but there was no time to answer. Blade in one hand and Witch in the other, the traveler continued to run through the streets, and while Alwera had little strength, now that Raaka wasn't holding her back, her weightless body could easily keep up with him. In theory, they were now fast enough to outrun any pursuers, and yet the guards remained stuck to their heels. For each of them that fell away due to exhaustion, a new group appeared from the joining streets, and soon, the city behind them was teeming with pursuers.

As they kept running away from the avalanche of guards, their group approached one of the tunnels in the vines protecting the city. From the other side, the traveler could clearly hear the sound of the waves, and seeing that their pursuers didn't show any signs of relenting, he decided to resort to more drastic measures. Taking his sword, he fixed the exit ahead with his gaze and swung the Fountain Blade across the wall, leaving Alwera wondering at his useless antics: The gate, too far away for his sword to reach, had remained completely unharmed, and she was just about to ask what he was doing when they entered the tunnel, passing below the vines that appeared so sturdy. Suddenly, a rumbling noise sounded behind her, and when Alwera turned her head, the ceiling of the tunnel had come down to block the way of their pursuers. Obviously, this had to be the work of the traveler's sword, and this realization made Alwera put aside her grudges to study the strange, metal feather for the first time. While she was reluctant to admit it, she would have loved to take a closer look then and there – if the traveler wouldn't have suddenly dispelled it.

Leaving the guards behind them to find a different route, the warehouses left and right of their group soon opened up to the water. Following the shore, a broad quay had been built next to the city wall, and from it branched countless vines that carried smaller piers far out onto the water. With the day now drawing closer to its end, every inch of free space was brimming with fishers unloading and carriers carrying, and still running at full speed, the traveler barely managed to screech to a halt before the rushing river they formed. Looking left and right, he tried to come up with an idea how to get past all those people, but in those few seconds he stood and thought, the crowd flowing ahead of them gradually slowed. Whispers and pointing limbs rose here and there as more and more people gripped the pendants of their goddess. Unfortunately, Raaka's glowing hair wasn't exactly inconspicuous.

"Those people are like fanatics," Alwera whispered to the traveler while trying to hide Raaka behind her as best as possible. "Although I can take care of them, are you really sure about rescuing your silly 'princess'? Just so you know, the ship *she* is held in belongs to Happy Harriet's. You can still change your mind."

"Happy who?"

Alwera sighed, not bothering to explain, and pulled out a strip of paper from her arm to jot down a string of runes. Holding it between index and middle finger, the traveler watched curiously as she waved it from side to side and in front of her face. At first, he didn't *see* anything happen, but then, the crowd in front of their group slowly stopped paying attention to them.

One after another, the fervent gazes slid off the Witch like she had suddenly turned into trash, but that wasn't all. As Alwera thrust out her hand, the quickening crowd suddenly parted, opening a small passage for them to pass.

"Why didn't you do that earlier?" the traveler asked in confusion. Couldn't they have easily avoided a chase through half of the city this way?

"This is just a cheap glamour spell," Alwera scoffed. "It does not work on people who are alert, and not on those that are already looking for you. Now get going, before it wears off." As if to prove her claim, a group of guards suddenly bent into the street behind them.

"There! Don't let them get away!" The traveler swallowed his complaints and hurriedly followed Alwera through the parting crowd. She continued to wave around her talisman the whole time they walked across the vines, her aversion spell keeping the people out of their way. Their pursuers, on the other hand, had no such protection, so when Alwera stopped in front of the slave galley, they had long fallen out of sight.

"This is it," she said and turned around to the traveler. "Do what you have to, but my spell will wear off in around a minute – time in which *I* will head to our escape ship. It is right down the pier." She pointed at *The Patchy* in the distance, and the traveler acknowledged with a nod before studying the sign dangling from the side of the slave galley, the same one Raaka was currently staring at. Happy Harriet's Helpful Human Resources, it said, and while the name wasn't familiar to him, Alwera seemed to have heard of them before – and so did the Witch.

"Alwera," Raaka asked in a voice somehow colder than usual, "what is a *slave ship* doing in *my* city?" But instead of an answer, her friend suddenly began to pull her away.

"I am *really* sorry, but we have no time for this, Raaka!"

"But–"

"*We are leaving!*" As Raaka was hauled off by Alwera, the traveler watched with a frown as they disappeared into the masses. Right before they did, however, Alwera turned around to ask a strange question. "You will not come back until your rescue is over, right?"

"Of course not!" he replied before shouting at the crowd around them. "Today is rescue day, everyone! Half the price for princess rescues! *Half the price I say!*" Unfortunately, no one reacted. Oh how he hated being ignored.

Clicking his tongue, someone else hurriedly called out to him from the crowd. "Cat-man!" It was Raaka, her shrinking face disappearing and appearing behind a forest of countless legs. "If I can't help the slaves myself, at least deal with the slavers for me!" Deal with the slavers? But she was already gone.

With a shrug, the traveler jumped off the quay and across the water where he landed directly on the slave galley's bowsprit. He could consider this request later. For now, he had to reach his princess – for the rescue had already begun!

THE BELLY OF THE BEAST

In theory, the traveler's plan was simple. Get into the ship, grab the princess, and get out again – except that it wasn't. Now that he stood on the bowsprit, he could see the guards spread all along the deck, and despite Alwera's spell, they, too, could see him clearly – or at least they came charging at him without asking questions.

The first attack was a storm of four daggers wielded by a boar-headed Spig, followed by a halberd swung by a towering Dzorok. Dancing around on the narrow bowsprit, the traveler evaded the latter before he jumped over the Spig's daggers by somersaulting over his head. Although the Spig instantly turned around, he only found a few feathers and his Dzorok companion who suddenly screamed. As the three-legged giant slumped down onto the deck, one leg bent at a clearly unnatural angle, the traveler appeared behind the guard's falling back.

"Oops," he said, "and here I thought two legs would be enough for a person to stand." The Spig charged at him in anger, but the result didn't change much compared to his first attack. No matter how often the guard swung his daggers, they only hit air or feathers until his large, curled tail was suddenly gripped tightly. The boar head of the Spig quickly turned, and he saw the traveler grinning a broad grin. "Bye bye!" With his tail pulled up high, the second guard flew overboard with a pitiful scream. A loud splash could be heard as the traveler dusted off his hands. Two of the guards were dealt with, but there were plenty of them left. By now, they had formed an orderly circle around him, so he decided to use his sword on them for the first time.

At the sight of the new danger, the guards hastily retreated a few steps. No one wanted to end up like their Dzorok colleague who still writhed on the floor. Among them, he had been the best fighter. "Quickly, call the boss!" While one of the guards ran off to call for help, the traveler cleared his throat, and for some reason, it made the people around him flinch. They looked way too pitiful as they gave him nervous stares, not like guards at all.

"Why don't you wait here for a while?" the traveler asked them and swung his sword, suddenly falling down and through the circular hole it had left. The guards gathered around it, all sharing baffled looks. What should they do? While they were still trying to answer that question, the traveler plummeted closer to his goal.

A round piece of deck hit the ground with a dull thud, and the traveler landed right on top of it. Rising from his crouch and dispelling his sword, he felt the musty air stroke heavily along his skin, just as suffocating as the darkness beyond the pillar of light falling around him. However, there was no shadow black enough to hide the grime and sweat from his eyes. The whole deck he stood in was covered in unwashed people, chains leading between them and then to the benches that stretched on into the dark.

Seeing that the floor was full of sleeping people, the traveler looked downwards and found a haggard human at his feet, or rather, below the round piece of deck he had landed on. The weight pressing down on the man must have been heavy, but not heavier than his exhaustion, so he didn't wake. Just like the others, he had to be a slave. What else would there be inside a slave ship?

Looking at that dreary sight, the traveler's hat lowered in silence as he extended his arms in a symbolic embrace. It was a merciful pose, a soft halo created behind him by the light descending from above, and if it wasn't for his black coat and suspiciously shadowed face, he could have almost passed for an angel.

Rustle, rustle.

At the sudden noise, the traveler's arms fell back to his sides, and he glanced to his right where a single slave scuttled closer in fascination. It was a sand-colored being similar to a spider, one of its six legs missing, but where a normal spider's head would grow rose a humanoid torso, bearing a heart-shaped spider head. However, even considering the soft tuft of hair growing on top, it barely reached the traveler's waist.

The small and at least slightly adorable slave stopped at the edge of the light and raised its head to look upwards. Obviously, it hadn't been fascinated by the traveler but with the hole in the ceiling above him, and the light from above reflected eight times in the row of its eight eyes, and once in the silky necklace dangling below its jaws.

A second of silence passed in which the slave stared at the light until it finally noticed the traveler. Their eyes met, and he gave a curt nod, then jumped from the person he was standing on and towards the head of the next. There was no time to care about anything else but the demon, so the little spider was left behind as he proceeded from forehead to forehead to arrive at the end of the narrow room. A huge drum stood on a raised dais, and behind it waited a wooden door only secured with a simple lock. It seemed that, with the slaves already chained to the benches, there was no need for more safety.

Taking out his sword, the traveler noticed a small sign hanging on the door and read the message written on it. "Staff room – Keep out the merchandise, keep locked, and, above all, keep smiling~! :-)" A silvery swing later, lock and sign were cut apart and fell to the floor, where his boots crushed the innocent smile to dust. He hated those obnoxious things.

After thrusting open the remains of the door, a small, smoky cabin came into view. Filled with narrow bunk beds, crates, colorful festoons made of cloth, and a small table with three sailors, the cabin was so full that it was difficult to see to the other side. On top of that, that smiling face from earlier was everywhere, on the festoons, on posters attached to the walls, and even the sailors, who had suddenly jumped up, wore little badges that carried it. Apparently, the traveler realized, it was the emblem of Happy Harriet's. What a weird company…

While the traveler had been looking around, the sailors had abandoned their game of cards for good and pulled out their weapons. "Who are you!? How'd ya get in there?!"

"Are you the slave traders?"

"Shut up!" one of them replied. "We're asking the questions 'ere, so tell us how ya got in there! Or we will make ya!" Seeing that the traveler didn't reply, the sailors started to awkwardly climb over the cluttered floor, somehow trying to attack him all at once.

"I take this as a yes." There was a silvery slash as the traveler swung his sword, and two of the sailors went sprawling lifelessly over the crates around them. They didn't show any injuries, but if someone were to look into their bodies, they would see that their hearts had been cleanly cut in two. After all, the Witch said that he should deal with the slavers – although one of them was still alive.

“W-wha–!” It was the same person who had shouted at him so rudely a moment ago, but now, there was nothing left of his aggressive attitude. Like a broken toy, he lay stammering on the floor, unable to move anything but his head. Wearing a kind smile, the traveler stepped closer to bend over him.

“Where is the rest of you?” he asked the last survivor who desperately tried to turn his head away, a futile attempt to escape the monster in front of him.

“T-t-they’re not here! We three were supposed to s-steer, and the rest wasn’t needed with all t-those guards around! B-believe me! Please, d-don’t–” The traveler stood up, and the slaver’s head slumped down. He was dead.

This was what the Witch had wanted, right? After all, Alwera had told him she was quite the caring person, and there was nothing more caring but to deal with an enemy painlessly. “What a waste, though,” he said as he left the three bodies behind and proceeded into the small stairway on the other side of the room. It was clean and tidy, exactly the opposite of the section the slaves were held in, and the same way that there was no dirt, there were no guards either. For some reason, they had stopped paying attention to him.

Deciding not to worry about it, the traveler took the stairs and arrived in the belly of the ship where a dense jungle of cargo greeted him. Crates and chests and bags carrying Happy Harriet's smiling emblem where everywhere, filled with precious spices and fabrics. The traveler, however, ignored all those worldly distractions, only focusing on the demon. After a short while of searching around the cargo hold, a small glade opened up in the crates in front of him, and there, surrounded by a circle drawn from square symbols, he finally found it.

"Oh, my princess!" he rejoiced in relief. "My jewel below the stars, guess who has come to save you!" The reaction he got wasn't as he expected, however. Yes, the demon *did* whip around with a growl, but it also tried to swipe at him with its claws before that weird circle repelled it. Wait… maybe this *was* the reaction he had expected? While the traveler continued to observe, the demon growled from time to time, revealing its obvious lack of sanity. When the traveler stared into its red eyes, the only thing he saw in them was hunger.

"Hmm, why does this sight feel so familiar…?" he mused left and right while he stared at the demon, trying for once to piece his memories back together. It seemed that he had known a way to overcome the current state of his demon. "But really," he sighed, "how did this even happen?"

While he couldn't ask the demon at the moment, one part of the answer likely lay in the strange circle that was trapping it. Written on a band of cloth spread on the floor, its square runes were a complete mystery to the traveler, but at the same time, he could tell that many of them matched those Alwera had used to remove Raaka's bracelet. This circle was Abjuration? While he had no idea how something meant to dispel magic could imprison a demon, if this was true, then Alwera was the one who had cast this circle. It was impossibly unlikely that there were more of her sort in this world, much more so on this little island. But why hadn't she told him about any of this?

Suspicious, the traveler stood up from where he had been kneeling and readied his blade, which caused the demon to retreat with a hiss. This was going to be interesting. Silver flashed, the air above the square runes flickered, and water shot into the room as the Fountain Blade cut all the way through the hole in the ship. Maybe he should have been a little more careful?

While that thought passed through his head, the demon already came flying. Without the barrier he had just destroyed, it was finally free, nothing stopping it from feasting on souls until it vomited. Nothing, except for the jagged, crimson runes that suddenly flashed up on its forehead. Grunting in pain, the demon fell to the floor despite his frenzy, but not without squashing the traveler below its weight. As he lost the grip on the Fountain Blade, it dissolved into thin air.

"Ugh, get off me, you lug," the traveler groaned, prompting the demon to spring up and attack once more. This time, however, it was the demon that suddenly found itself pinned to the floor, an arm twisted behind its back. As the traveler sat on top of the struggling animal, he suddenly pierced his hand towards its heart. There was no blood, however, just crimson light where his fingers met gray-purple scales, and soon, his arm had disappeared up to the shoulder inside the now frozen demon.

“Let’s see,” the traveler murmured as he searched around the demon’s back like a deep drawer, whimpers reaching his ears each time he changed direction. Although it only took a few seconds, it felt like hours until his hand finally gripped something squirming. “There they are!” the traveler said and pulled out his arm, in his hand the souls the demon had stored inside its heart. The two beings, resembling a mix of jellyfish and octopus, squeaked weakly between his fingers as their glowing tentacles trailed like red ribbons in the air.

“It worked? It worked! But why are there only two? My princess, either you are too greedy or too stupid, keeping so little lunch.” The souls in one hand, the demon’s head in the other, the traveler pulled open its mouth, but it wasn’t meant to be that easy. The beast had started to thrash around again. “Stop it, you idiot!” the traveler cursed as they struggled through the cargo hold, but eventually, the demon’s mouth was forced open, followed by a stuffing of souls down its throat. Just like that, the previously frenzied beast slumped down without so much as a stir, and the traveler slowly pulled out his hand. His whole sleeve was covered in slobber. “Ewww,” he said, but although he fiercely tried to wipe it on the demon, the drool didn't come off at all. "Is this supposed to be the punishment for my crimes? Worlds, we *really* don't have the time for this now!"

Pushing the matter of a new coat back to later, the traveler started to drag the unconscious demon away, up the stairs, past the staff room, and towards the exit which he swiftly kicked open. The upper deck outside was completely deserted, the suns already battling for space at the horizon, and as their orange and green rays reached out, they painted the vines and the maze in darkening shades of color. But the traveler didn't stop to appreciate the beautiful sight. Gripping the demon's horns with both hands, he dragged him over the threshold with a thud.

"What the Den are *you* doing here?" someone suddenly said behind his back, and the demon's head hit the floor as the traveler simply let go.

"What *I* am doing?" he asked in return, spinning around with a bow and a tip of his hat. "I am rescuing a princess, dear villain!" Straightening, the shape of a three-legged giant came into view ahead, a bluish steel mountain glowing a dull gray in the sunsset. The traveler grinned happily at the sight. "Are you, perhaps, here for our final showdown?"

"You know what," Yarok replied after a second of silence, "I don't even want to understand. Just be reasonable and hand over that demon." The ship shook as he swung his hammer up with one hand to point it at the traveler. "Or you will regret it!"

"Ahh!" The traveler playfully put a hand to his head as if he could faint any moment. "This is exactly what I meant! Why didn't you just admit that I was right. The youths these days, so impatient!" Although it was a cheap taunt, it still seemed to hit its mark, and a screech rang out from Yarok's clenching gauntlets. It was like music to the traveler's ears. Of course, there was a reason he was so unfazed by all of this. While he hadn't exactly expected for his demon to be kidnapped, after he had learned about that, it at least wasn't shocking to find Yarok involved in this little ploy. After all, no one in his right mind would let a demon run through their city *and* offer someone a free place to stay. His friendliness had just been too suspicious. Still smiling, the traveler now spread his arms wide, the dull silver of his blade reappearing in his hands. "I'm sorry to disappoint you, Yarok, but I have just noticed myself." His eyes mirthfully sparkled beneath his dark hat as they stared at each other. This was his answer. "I am *totally* unreasonable."

CONFRONTATION

As Alwera emerged from the crowds filling the quay, she stowed away the enchanted paper in her hand and led Raaka towards *The Patchy*. At the sight of the unknown ship that they would apparently use to escape, Raaka cast an uncertain glance at her friend. "Are you sure about traveling over water?"

Alwera answered as she walked up the plank, "How else would we get off this island? I am sure I can endure the ocean for a little while." Raaka gave a hesitant nod, not quite convinced that Alwera really would be able to suppress her fear of the water. "It will be our smallest problem on this journey anyway." Hearing that ominous sentence, Raaka was just about to ask for an explanation when a small metal crab fell from the masts above and interrupted her.

"Captaaaain," it squeaked loudly, "I think the customers have arrived!" Seconds later, Karoly appeared inside the door to the ship. While those people on her deck looked like strangers to her, she trusted Shiny's assessment completely. However, the same was true for her own judgment which told her that her customers seemed somewhat hurried.

"Are there any problems I should know of?" Karoly asked as her gaze swept along the crowded piers, and of course, she quickly spotted the guards that tried to get past the masses and search the ships lying in the harbor. They were still quite far away though.

"Problems?" Alwera asked innocently. "There are no problems if we get out of here quickly. Just leave as soon as possible."

Snorting, Karoly turned around to do just that. "ASSES UP AND READY THE SHIP! IT'S BACK TO THE SEA, EVERYONE!" Her crew quickly clamored up the stairs while Karoly herself took the wheel on the aftercastle, the raised deck at the end of the ship. "Although the pay's good, how can there be trouble already?" she muttered on her way up before glaring at Raaka and Alwera. They were still blocking the center of the deck. "You! At least have the decency to stay out of the way while we're working!"

"Yes, yes," Alwera appeased as she slowly moved to the railing, content with looking at the slave galley the traveler had long disappeared into. Raaka came up next to her, her expression glum, so she tried to cheer her up a little. "I am sure you will feel better after some time passes." But Raaka, too, only stared at the slave galley, just for different reasons. If her eyes were weapons, it would have sunk already.

This way, each of them stayed silent although there were many things to talk about, and sunsdown approached quickly. The crew behind them took care of their preparations, while the guards on the vine-held piers slowly pushed closer. Suddenly,

Raaka asked a worried question. “Will Cat-man even make it in time?”

“I do not know either. We can only wait, can’t we?” Although Alwera showed a smile to Raaka, she didn’t feel it at all. Even though she hadn’t told him about it, she was sure that the Forgetful wouldn’t make it through her circle, the one that had been put up inside the slave galley. If he wasted too much time trying to break through, that annoying Godly wouldn’t make it in time – or maybe he would simply decide to abandon that despicable demon. She would already be happy as long as she didn’t have to travel with both of those monsters at the same time.

Looking forward to the future no matter what happened, Alwera stood at the railing until *The Patchy* slowly started to set out. The guards were too slow, and as an added bonus for the success of her ruse, a towering shape lumbered up the slave galley in front of them.

“Haha, I cannot believe it, is that Sir Yarok?!” Alwera was clearly excited. “Can I finally see a fight?!” Raaka, who stood next to her, gave an exasperated eye-roll at the attitude of her friend. Some things never changed. “Those are prime seats, Raaka! Mark my words!” Saying so, Alwera leaned forward so she wouldn’t miss a second of the ensuing battle, leaving it to Raaka to keep her from falling overboard. The door to the slave galley was finally kicked open, but Alwera didn’t like what she was seeing. The Forgetful wasn’t as alone as she had thought. “W-whaaaaat?!”

"I am *totally* unreasonable." Opposing Yarok, a dark coat fluttered in the sunsdown winds, a broad hat crowning smiling eyes and a relaxed stance. "This play, let's get it started, my villain!" However, Yarok didn't need an invitation and already rushed forward explosively. The deck shook three times before the spear end of his hammer was thrust at the traveler, but he barely evaded. "Close one, but not quite!"

"You little!" Switching his grip, Yarok swung a circle with his weapon, planning to smash his enemy aside, but again, the traveler narrowly escaped by bending backwards. The hammer harmlessly passed above his face, but he *did* almost lose his hat. Another swing that made the deck groan, and another miss. "Stop! Fidgeting!"

While the twitchiness of his opponent clearly annoyed Yarok, as an experienced warrior, he simply channeled that feeling into his attacks. His swings got faster, stronger, heavier until the traveler couldn't keep up anymore. The lump of iron that Yarok called a hammer finally smashed into his side, but Yarok's shout was not a happy one. His weapon had only scattered feathers.

"This again!" His anger echoed clearly from his helmet. "Can't you come up with anything else?!" Having lost track of his opponent, the armor-clad giant whipped around but only found the unconscious demon still laying at the galley's entrance.

"Up here I am, world! Look at me!" Reflexively following the voice, Yarok really looked up, but the moment he did, the traveler crashed down into his big helmet, clinging to it with arms and legs. Two glinting eyes suddenly stared at him through his visor, and a playful whisper, with a tinge of malice, echoed inside his helmet. "*You want to see another trick? And here I thought this was already too much for you!*" With that, the eerie eyes disappeared as fast as they arrived, and two silver lines flashed through the arriving night as the traveler flipped off Yarok's shoulders and through the air. "Here you go! How do you like it?"

At the same time the traveler landed, a clattering sound came from around Yarok's feet. The sturdy armor around his arms had simply fallen off, revealing the scars on the bony skin plates below. While the traveler's grin sparkled with self-satisfaction, Yarok seemed quite confused. "How did you–"

"Sir Yaaaaroooooook!" A happy but slightly desperate voice suddenly cut him off. "You can doooo iiit!" At once, the traveler's grin turned into a frown, and his head turned towards their escape ship. Seeing what was happening there, he was so angry that a vein appeared on his forehead.

"WHAT ARE YOU DOING, YOU NEWSPAPER!?" He stomped with his feet like a petulant child, not in small part because the atmosphere had been completely destroyed. "AT LEAST CHEER FOR *ME*, NOT FOR *MY OPPONENT!?* YOU WASTE OF PAPER! YOU SHOULD CHEER FOR *ME!*"

Of course, Alwera had watched their match from the start, hoping that Yarok would manage to keep the traveler busy until *The Patchy* was gone. When it wasn't going well, however, she tried to support him from afar with cheering. Still, at the traveler's angry rebuke, she paused for a moment.

"Youu are tootally riiight! …Go, Sir Yarok, go! Do not disappoint me!"

While the traveler was speechless, the giant in question looked even more confused at the sudden cheers. When he finally followed the traveler's gaze and found an unknown ship carrying Lady Alwera, he was shocked. When he heard that she went missing, he had thought someone abducted her, so why, after everything that happened, was she leaving on her own volition? But as ridiculous as that was, that wasn't the worst: Next to Alwera stood someone else. Below his helmet, the blood drained from Yarok's face as he recognized the Witch, who was so important in their defense against the Edge. Why was *she* escaping too? As Yarok's gaze fell back onto the traveler, he quickly found the answer to all of his questions. "Y-you!" he screamed as he ran towards the traveler, the grip of his hammer screeching under the pressure of his two huge hands. "You, you, YOU!" Yarok's hammer swung down a thousand times, splintering the deck again and again until its edges started glowing with heat. “HOW DARE YOU!!” Screams coming from the slaves below, the planks of the deck broke, the railing splintered, but the traveler dodged it all, dancing like a feather in the wind.

“What should I say, my villain?" he quipped while Alwera cheered in the background and the ship around them slowly turned into a ruin. “Would you let me off if I told you that I’m just borrowing the Witch for a while?” Another swing that made the air burn was his answer. The traveler, acknowledging that this was a little more dangerous than a random earth-worm in a plain, glanced at *The Patchy* that had slowly started to move out. It would be better if he hurried.

“I guess it is time,” he said as Yarok took yet another swing, the last one he would ever take – because his hammer suddenly fell apart. Still mid-attack, most of it raced over the remains of the railing, where its heavy head sank a random ship in the distance. Because his weapon had been cut apart by the traveler, Yarok instantly retreated. After everything that happened, he had gone way past angry and reached a level of hate that sent steam hissing through the gap of his visor.

“Alright,” Yarok said with a voice like the calm before the storm. “I don’t need a weapo–”

“Ah! How terrible,” the traveler interrupted, currently standing right outside melee range. “I am really sorry, my villain, but–" His tone was so deeply dismissive that it finally made Yarok notice the bad feeling he'd had since the first time his armor was cut. But it was too late. His legs suddenly gave out, all three of them at once.

"W-what?!" Although he tried to move them just the same way he would normally, they didn't budge an inch.

"I'm so sorry," the traveler continued, "that I don't have the time to finish our play." He gave an apologetic bow while Yarok was frozen in shock. With his legs sprawled out at random angles, he looked a bit like an octopus with three legs.

"What is this!?" the giant shouted at the traveler. "What have you done?!"

"Oh, Yarok." The traveler shook his head. "One way or another, all villains atone for their sins, believe me. While you ought to consider this your punishment, you don't have to worry." There was a chuckle as he picked up the demon. "If I did it right, the nerves in your legs will grow back together. It isn't permanent. Otherwise, how could we continue this later?"

"La…ter?" Yarok's voice broke. If he did it right? How ridiculous. Not only could he not move his legs, the abducted demon and even Raaka had escaped. It was simply too much to stomach at once.

"Yes, later." Casually, the traveler stepped in front of him with a nod, a dim shape in the twilight. "Why don't you let me tell you something, as reward for our little fight?" Yarok was too shocked to answer, but despite that, the traveler leaned in like he wanted to share a secret. In this moment, he somehow managed to tower over the battered giant despite being the smaller one. "Remain knowing that this world, and all others, are just a stage to me, and you and everything within just faithful actors. Why do you think I'm traveling with a demon? Isn't it obvious? How should I, without obstacles to overcome, without actors to overcome them with, ever find fulfillment? And so – why should I kill *you* just because you tried to play your allotted part? That would be too cruel."

Yarok, dumbfounded, simply stared at the lunatic in front of him, flinching when he leaned even closer. "No… Instead, *please, I beg of you.*" Pleading whispers trickled sweetly down the giant's ears. "Should we ever meet again, please entertain me some more."

Leaving that last sentence, the traveler disappeared from view, and Yarok's back crashed down onto the broken planks of the deck. He had lost all his will to move. *This* was supposed to be punishment? How laughable. Compared to what would await him next, even death would have been a welcome way out.

THE UNCERTAIN FUTURE

After dealing with Yarok, the traveler hurried straight back to the bow of the slave ship. With the demon on his shoulder, he hid around a heap of broken crates where he noticed all too clearly that he hadn't escaped yet. By now, night had fallen completely, and the vines and piers leading to the slave ship were covered in loads of soldiers. Certainly, they must have seen him fight with Yarok, but their torchlit faces still seemed determined to stop anyone who wanted to leave. There was no way he could deal with all of them in time, especially considering the Witch's outlandish request. At that point, however, a high voice suddenly called out to him over the waves.

"Hey, killjoy!" It was Alwera. "Seems you will not make it in time, so nice knowing you!" Whipping around, the traveler saw *The Patchy* heading for the ocean. The ship was already some distance away, slowly approaching the only channel leading through the vines around the island and out onto the sea. Of course, this was good because the guards couldn't stop it anymore, but at the same time, this meant he couldn't board either. "See you sooon~!" Alwera taunted again as *The Patchy* picked up more speed.

"That walking newspaper," the traveler cursed with a glare, and stormed towards the side of the slave galley not bordering the pier. "Once I get my hands on her, she can count herself lucky to end up as kindling." From the circle trapping his demon, over her unnecessary cheering, and up to these taunts, everything about the Papersnip screamed betrayal. But, by far, the worst was that she hadn't even cheered for him! With a loud splash, problem number two, also known as princess demon, went flying into the harbor water. So what if the piers were blocked? Then they would simply have to swim. With a look at his drool-stained sleeve, he jumped off the deck, and the next moment, he broke through the frothing waves to dive after the sinking demon. He needed a bath anyway.

A few gasps later, he broke the surface once more, now carrying the demon. "Ah, on second thought, maybe *this* is the real punishment for my crimes." Cursing, the traveler started to swim, spitting out loads of harbor water only for his clothes to suck them up again. Soon, the brim of his hat got so heavy that it blocked his sight, but he stubbornly pulled the demon after him. What he couldn't see that way, however, was that the ship was too fast and they too slow, the main reason being the princess that pulled him down like the stone she was. "I swear, once you wake up, you will go on a diet." Of course, he didn't get an answer.

Meanwhile, Alwera, standing on the dry and safe deck of *The Patchy*, was relieved. In the end, all her plans had worked out: Goodbye Godly, goodbye demon – See you never!

"No!" someone shouted next to her, as if to reject her self-satisfied thoughts. "We have to pull them out!" Hearing that, Alwera's mind suddenly ground came to a halt. Naturally, the one who had spoken was Raaka, Raaka who always saved everything and everyone. She couldn't deny her outright, so she at least tried to stall as much as possible.

"Ah, you are right! O-of course you are right, let me get a rope, and–"

"There's no time for that!" Before Alwera could make up more excuses, Raaka had waved a hand, and a small wave towered up to carry their new companions towards *The Patchy*. The water washed them up the hull where the traveler managed to grip the edge of the deck and slap the demon onto the planks like a wet towel. Raaka flinched for a moment, recognizing *what* it was that had just landed there – not that it kept her from running over to check when she saw that he was unconscious.

Breathing heavily, the traveler pulled himself onto the deck to lie down on the planks as well. Although he had only swam a few dozen meters, it felt like years since he had jumped from the deck of the slave galley, and now, he was completely drenched. A laugh escaped him as the dirty harbor water slowly gathered to a puddle around him. When was the last time he had felt so excited? But then, a shadow fell over his face, and his grin faded.

"You are blocking the moonslight," he said coldly, glaring at Alwera who stood bent over him. Following his words, she nodded once and quickly took a step aside, now blocking even more of the light. "What's your problem, newspaper?!" the traveler shouted at her, finally losing it. "First you lie to me, then you cheer for the wrong person, and now this! How about you simply keep your mouth shut forever?!"

"I think I am the only one who decides who I cheer for!" Alwera huffed in response. "Such a pity Yarok didn't rough you up some more! I wonder how the fight would have gone without that disgusting translocation spell of yours!"

"Come here, you outdated flyer! I'll turn you into shreds!"

"Ha! I want to see you try!"

As they continued to throw insults at each other, captain Karoly, doing her best to bring them through the vines around the harbor, finally reached the end of her patience. The tea in her pipe almost spilled, so forcefully did she point at the demon lying on her deck. "DEMONS DON'T TAKE SHIPS! WOULD SOMEONE PLEASE EXPLAIN WHAT'S GOING ON?!"

""No!"" Alwera and the traveler replied at once, continuing their squabbling right after. Karoly, baffled, stared at them for a second before slowly but firmly placing her pipe back where it belonged. She could indeed only watch as her new customers continued to argue. These were the times she hated the business codex.

"CAPTAIN! The vines!"

The shout made Karoly turn away from her strange customers, and oh, she really didn't like what she was seeing there. "BOBLOB!" she shouted down to the mechanic who was somewhere in the depths of the ship. "MOVE YOUR FAT ASS AND GET SHINY UP AND RUNNING!" Her tone was so serious that Alwera interrupted their argument, and suddenly, she and the traveler tried to beat each other to the bow of the ship to see what was happening. They arrived at the same time and instantly recognized the problem: The vines in the water had begun to move, and the channel that led out of the city was narrowing by the second. The thorny greens were like the tentacles of a giant octopus as they shot up around *The Patchy*, determined to hold the ship in their grip. If this went on, they wouldn't manage to escape. "BLOBBY, GOD DAMN IT!" Karoly hysterically shouted over the deck, trying to steer past the vines springing up left and right. "WHAT IS TAKING YA SO LONG!!?" The crew had already started to pull out their blades and hack away at the vines, but it didn't do much.

"What's this?" the traveler complained. "They don't want to let us go? I don't like clingy characters..." Alwera, who stood at his side, almost dropped the papers she had pulled out for some reason, starting to shake him left and right.

"Keep your dumb lines to yourself and do something!" By now, the thin strip of blue leading out of the vines was barely large enough to let their ship through – but it wouldn't be that way for much longer.

"Alright, alright," the traveler replied reluctantly and summoned his sword, slicing away at the vines just like the rest of the crew. Some of the tendrils were almost as thick as their ship, but although whole swathes of them were cut off by his blade, their chunks simply regrew the moment they fell into the water. Each second, their thorns came closer and closer to the hull of *The Patchy*, threatening to grasp it for good. At some point, the traveler simply had enough. "Screw this," he muttered, turning around his quill-like sword as if he was about to write something with it. The vines had now enclosed most of the ship, so this was the best choice to get rid of them. He only hoped that this would go better than last time... Shaking off the thought, the traveler started to speak, "Remembering the Source, this nameless wretch dons his allotted role: The Poet who Omits–" Just at that moment, a wave of blue light swept around the ship, and he almost fell overboard as the deck lurched up into the air. The vines trapping them had been shattered apart, and the sea that came into view glowed an icy blue so bright that even his dark coat appeared almost white. Cloth fluttered wildly as the traveler, no, the Poet whipped around and saw what had happened on the far side of the ship. And, oh, how he didn't like what he saw there: His demon, holding a lifeless Witch.

A few moments earlier, when *The Patchy* had started to evade the approaching vines, Raaka had been sitting right next to the unconscious demon. Although the crew was shouting and running all around her, she didn't react to the budding chaos and showed no intention to move at all. Rooted to the spot, she simply stared at the monster in front of her. When it had been thrown over the railing, right onto the deck at her feet, all she could think of was that Tinton had been right, and there really was a demon here. Like everyone else, she had heard the stories about them, even seen her fair share of evidence during the recent Harvest she had witnessed with Ellie. Firsthand, she had seen how cruel they could be, torturing innocents and guilty people wherever they went, but as she looked at the drenched form of the person in front of her, she wasn't afraid. Her only thought was to help him. Leaning closer with that determination, she tried to find out why he wasn't waking up. Unfortunately, she knew next to nothing about demon physiology, but he clearly had a nose, so she assumed that he likely had to breathe as well. Leaning in even farther to check, Raaka noticed how the faint smell of sulfur grew stronger around her. It was a scent underlined by a faint trace of sweetness, and it washed away the last of her doubts that this was indeed a real demon and not just something that happened to look that way.

Relieved at feeling air flow from his chest, she struggled a moment before she turned the demon's large, square face towards her. With her free hand, she lifted up his lids, only to see that he didn't have pupils in the first place! Rather than eyes, what sat in his face were like two smoldering coals burning with a red glow. For a moment, she stared into their scorching flames, and so she didn't miss how the left eye rapidly changed to an icy blue. It was a vibrant, captivating color, and as she stared into it, the hue resonated deeply inside of her. The color felt just so... familiar. Before she could get closer, however, the demon coughed, and a gush of stinky harbor water rushed straight into her face.

Recoiling, Raaka quickly cleaned her eyes, and once she was done, she suddenly noticed the chaos reigning over the ship: She saw vines growing left and right of the deck, so high they towered above the masts. She saw Cat-man hacking off tendril after tendril along with the rest of the crew, and the captain trying to evade the growing obstacles. However, she also saw that it was too little, too late. If no one did anything, their ship would be shredded to bits!

With a last lingering look at the strange demon, Raaka rose to her feet and dashed off towards the aftercastle. Up the stairs and past the captain, she ran full speed until she hit her knees against the hard railing. The situation felt so urgent that she hadn't bothered to slow down, but despite that, she suddenly froze at the sight sprawling past the water. There lay the city she was about to desert, painfully reminding her of all the things she was about to leave behind. She saw the harbor, the people on the quay staring at her. She saw the vine wall, protecting the infirmary where she had treated the sick, the market, where at least the smiles of the people had made up for the dwindling supplies, and Liam, Tinton, Kyta. "What am I doing?" Raaka whispered, hesitating for a moment. Did she really want to let the Edge destroy all of this? As if in reply to her feelings, a deep, otherworldly voice suddenly spoke up behind her.

The time to doubt is over, my lady. You don't have to be afraid. No matter what, I will never leave you again.

Tears rolled from Raaka's eyes as she turned around and looked up at the person bent over her.

When the demon ripped open his eyes, it was like he had finally reached air after a long dive. His head looked left, then right, his vision shifting between blurry and clear as he studied the deck of the unknown ship he was on. Strange green things wormed into the sky on all sides, and dark shades, people, ran around while water sprayed down on all of them. Where it hit his skin, he felt cool and comfortable, and only then, he noticed: All the hunger, all the greed, were suddenly gone, only the pain, still fresh in his mind, reminding of them. Strangely relieved, he reveled in the calm silence while his body started to move all on its own. Like in a dream, he watched it stand up and lumber over to the back of the ship, always following a strange thread of lightning that spanned through the air and ended at his goal. It was up the stairs, a small girl, alone and forgotten as she stared out at the sea. When he saw her back against the slate blue ocean, his heart bloomed the same way as when he ate a soul, and somehow, for some reason, he couldn't help but feel like all of this had happened before.

The time to doubt is over, my lady.

It was his mouth that had spoken, but not his voice coming from it, and yet, he merely listen to himself addressing the fragile girl.

You don't have to be afraid. No matter what, I will never leave you again.

Slowly, the girl turned around, and when she looked up, her tears flashed up like gems in the moonslight. "Really?" she asked weakly, about to shatter at any moment, and he and not he, the demon and not the demon, answered with a smile. After his big hands gently turned his master back onto the sea, his soft touch stayed to support her – like it had done so long ago.

Confused yet relieved, Raaka didn't resist when she was softly turned back towards the camp. The stranger behind her was right. The time to doubt was over, no matter how much it hurt. She had made her decision. For the last time, she fixed her eyes onto Merai, trying to preserve it all into her mind. In the end, she couldn't protect this place against the Edge. Were the things she had done here even helpful in the end? The deck swayed for a moment, but the hand still resting on her back kept her from falling overboard. It felt like a strong hand, ready to hold her weight, and taking comfort in that knowledge, Raaka finally lifted her arms over the railing. While she would need time to think about all of this, now was the time to act. The former slave girl, closer to other people than to herself, entered the spotlight at the edge of the railing and drew a large rune with glowing fingers. It was a spiral intersected by two circles.

To Tide, to what gifts and takes, I offer myself.

With a humming noise, the rune flashed up before shattering to dust, sparkling enchantingly blue as it started to circle around her. Where it converged, the fragments formed countless smaller runes, flitting in and out of existence, and for once, Raaka was thankful for the visions that came as she guided the spell. In front of her inner eye, she saw fierce waves, calm waves, endless floating, bubbling geysers, rushing rivers, more and more and more, until Merai, her city, her *sanctuary*, was finally gone from her view. Outside her mind, behind her focused face, was the demon, standing like a rock to support her on the swaying deck, all up till the thick vines had enveloped them completely. The last light shining through their closing gaps were his eyes and her hair, mirroring the color of the runes.

Suddenly, the world had turned dark. A single second had passed since Raaka had started, but it felt like forever before she saw the last memory Tide forced upon her: It was a gray, eye-sized pebble sinking into a dark abyss, doomed to search the ends of the ocean until the ends of time. She felt its loneliness, its longing, and could relate to its bitterness in her very own parting. By the time her amber eyes opened again, the ship had stopped, and the world outside had been hidden by vines. Just in the gaps here and there, she could see glimpses of people standing on the harbor, and for a moment, she imagined Tinton and Kyta, waving at her. A single gleaming tear fell from her eye, its sparkling light rippling out as a blinding wave of blue that shattered the thick vines around them. Water sprayed, wood flew everywhere, and a glowing wave carried *The Patchy* to safety.

Seeing the world once more, Raaka collapsed, the water falling from the sky mingling with the tears on her face. Her heart was hurting, her lungs were burning, and then, Tide took what was due. The last thing she saw before everything went black was her city, her life's work, racing away into the distance. And by the time the demon caught her, the tears were still running down her cheeks.

Shortly after the flash of light, *The Patchy* crashed back into the ocean, far away from the maze and from Merai. The traveler still stood at the bow of the ship, taking in the scene that presented itself to his eyes: The back of his demon, bent over a lifeless body.

"You monster!" Alwera's almost hysterical voice rang out, already rushing over. *"What have you done to her!?"* The traveler silently followed in her wake, up the stairs where he saw the back of his demon turned towards the sea. Visible in his arms were the limbs of the Witch, dangling like a puppet with cut strings. He answered without turning around.

Who are you? Leave us alone.

Alwera, just about to lunge at him, was suddenly pulled back. "No," the Poet asked as he lifted his sword. "Who are you?" The air was creaking ominously around him, like glass that was afraid of breaking. He wasn't amused at all. "Who are you, and what have done to my demon?"

The person in question slowly turned around, and the Poet's arm trembled slightly when the demon raised his opening eyes. What was supposed to be red was now an icy blue.

EPILOGUE

A MANY LEGGED WITNESS

Inside a moving cave made of wood, with no air to breathe and no light to see, sat a single spider. And although she was lonely, she wasn't alone: A crowd of strange creatures were trapped along with her, sitting and swaying in rows that went back and forth in a steady rhythm. In the beginning, she, too, had been a part of their ranks until her shackles slid from her thin, aching arms, and since that day, she constantly hid under the wooden squares everyone was sitting on, waiting and waiting. After all, there was nothing else she could do here. Nothing but longingly remember.

She hadn't always been here. Before they came to this strange place, before her mother traded her for round disks of metal, they had been living in a forest of rocky trees so thick they carried even the endless sky. It had been a sturdy and beautiful place, one she had thought they would stay in forever. And yet, now she sat here, only five legs instead of six, and waited while the others worked. Waiting for what? She didn't know...

After a while, the little spider turned her heart-shaped head downward and fixed her eyes onto her necklace. It was just a small circle, woven from silky thread and with strings spanned across its center, but although simple, it was still special to her. This necklace had been created by her mother, and now the threads of this parting gift were the only thing that still connected them. Well, maybe not the only thing.

As the spider plucked the strings spanned in the pendant's circle, a quiet sound spread through the air which she could only feel by its pull on her hair. It was a type of sound that was at least as special as the necklace itself: *Sahidi.* Her name.

Pulling the strings another time, she reveled in the feeling of their sounds stroking against her body, something she had never experienced in her old home. Sound didn't exist there, so it always felt like a novelty when she encountered one. Suddenly, a two-legger sitting on the wood above her fell down with a thud. Right next to her, it tried to stand up but was too weak, and shortly after, someone approached to motivate it with kicks. Sahidi retreated deeper into the shadows, watching in silence. It was always so hard to guess what was going on in this place and inside the creatures around her she had never seen before. Her mother had even warned her to not be surprised about every little thing, but she simply couldn't help it. Take sound, for example. Back home, no one could talk, and if something had to be recorded or shared, it was written down. Only the Sethari, her own people, were an exception, speaking by using links of thread. Understandably, after thinking so for all her short life, she had needed *days* to stop gaping at those weird mouths most of the people here had.

Sahidi watched the exhausted two-legger be dragged away and thought once more that it was quite a strange place she had landed up in. After a while of waiting, and sure that no one had noticed her, she decided to settle down for a break and skip some time. Pulling her remaining legs close to her body, her attention receded, senses stilling until they could barely track the movements of those around her. Maybe when she awoke, her mother would have come back to hold her. Yes… Maybe everything had just been a bad dream…

As Sahidi rested, she vaguely felt the swaying below her claws get weaker. The noises around her retreated, becoming a quiet snoring, a sound that somehow made her feel at ease. But then, she suddenly felt something she didn't know.

Snapping out of her rest, Sahidi sneaked out of her hiding spot and looked up to the source of the sound, almost out of reflex. Instantly, light stabbed at her eight black eyes, a brilliant pillar that descended from above, and her gazes fixed on the hole that was its source. Spellbound, she stepped closer, and for a second, she simply stared at the freedom beyond – until her sight fell down towards the *something* that stood right beneath.

It was similar to those two-leggers but slightly different. At about twice her height, a strange mushroom sat on its head and shimmered in the light while drenching the rest of the body below in darkness. From it, two eyes sharp as fangs glinted at her, causing her to freeze instinctively. Something told her that it was best to play dead in front of this being, and apparently, it was the right call to make. The thing left her after giving an approving nod, but she observed it the whole time it disappeared, just to make sure. Whew! What a relief.

Afraid of and yet thankful to her dark savior, Sahidi stepped up to the wooden walls of the cave. It felt like the start of a long journey as she brought her claws over the corner, walked across the ceiling and to the edge of the hole. Fresh wind stroked over the hairs on her face. Freedom.

With a last look downwards at the people sleeping in the darkness, she swung herself up and into the light.

As her five good legs touched down on the wood outside, she had to shield her eyes against the blinding light. This way, she noticed a little late that she had been wrong. Instead of freedom, she was greeted by a ring of two-leggers staring at her like she was a ghost. They looked awfully like guards, and all guards were dangerous. While the people around her stared at her, she quickly decided to make a fast getaway between their legs, but was soon cut short. The wooden ground abruptly found an end, and beyond its edge waited a lot of water, with waves like those that had ripped off her leg. There was no escaping this way, so she turned around to find another, but by now, the guards had woken from their stupor. And Sahidi knew: If they were to catch her, she would end up back where she started, in the wooden cave. Reluctantly, she glanced at the waves below. Then, she simply jumped over the railing.

As gravity pulled the spider-like creature towards the wet, the soldiers all bent over the railing to stare after it. Because this was the wrong side of the ship, it seemed like it wouldn't reach the piers on the other side, ending up drowning in the dirty waters. But suddenly, a thread shot from Sahidi's hands, swinging her around a nearby warehouse and onto the vines holding up the harbor. The guards on the slave galley all rubbed their eyes. Should they stay here or chase after the spider? 'Protect the cargo and the ship,' they had said, but did this thing count as cargo as well? The guards all shared a look, still remembering the scary intruder they would need to face otherwise. "E-everyone! After that spider!"

Swinging from thread to thread, along the posts of the tents and between towering stones, Sahidi quickly got away from the frightening waves. She received many gazes as she flew past the people below, but none of them seemed keen on following her. She knew, however, that it was only a matter of time – guards were persistent and dangerous. They had always been that way when they went stealing.

After using her threads for what felt like hours, Sahidi lowered onto the ground, her aching arms too exhausted to continue. Around her were only tents and no one in sight, so she simply slumped down where she was. She had no clue how long she had been in that wooden cave, but she could clearly feel the traces it had left on her body. In the past, she would have still been able to keep going.

Pulling in her legs, she slept once more, and in her dreams, the cloth of the tents around her was replaced by threads, by her old home, where her mother put her to sleep, and where the stranger who had freed her watched over them from the stars. In the end, however, a dream was just that: A dream. Sahidi awoke, and there was no trace of the rocky trees or her mother's soft touch. Only alien tents.

For a moment, she looked up at the suns and came up with the idea to go right back to sleep. She could do so for quite a long time, and in a few moons, maybe everything around her would have turned for the better. The thought had just crossed her mind when a familiar tune suddenly started to tug on the strands of her hair, a song she thought she would never hear again. It was a melody of her mother.

Distracted from her bleak thoughts, Sahidi carefully began to sneak through the gaps in the tents, across streets and around corners until the melody was just a step away. In an empty alley, right at the wall that blocked its end, she found the song's source and hurried closer, expecting to see her mother searching for her. But there was no one there, which hurt a little… Quite a lot, actually.

What lay there in the dirt by her claws instead was a harp spun of thread. No one was playing it, and yet its soundless melody echoed in Sahidi's mind. Like her necklace, she recognized it as a parting gift crafted by her mother, this one, however, shouldn't be here. It belonged to her elder brother who… had been left behind. How, by the winged, did it get here? As Sahidi stared at the harp, it suddenly stopped playing.

Sahidi.

She jumped back and looked around, but the dead end was as empty as it could get.

Sahidi!

She turned back to the harp lying right in front of her and picked it up, surprised how light it was despite being larger than her. The whole time, its strings continued to pluck themselves, and again and again she heard her name although she wasn't connected to it. Confused, Sahidi spun a thread between her hand and the harp, whispering through it.

"Brother?"

Take the harp and leave!

The voice of her brother sounded quite urgent, but at the same time, another noise came from Sahidi's back. She quickly focused back on her surroundings and saw three guards standing at the entrance of the dead end she was in. What a stupid mistake to not pay attention to her back eyes!

Leave!

The harp didn't need to tell her. As soon as Sahidi spotted the guards, she hurried up the wall in front of her, across the shaky tents, and through the streets leading from there. However, her pursuers stubbornly clung to her back, chasing her until exhaustion came back to slow her steps. If this went on, they would surely catch her – but she didn't want to end up in that cave again!

Go left!

At that moment, her brother suddenly spoke, once more ripping her from her plight, and with his help, she started to properly navigate through the confusing warren made of tents. The guards fell back a little but still kept chasing her all the way until sunset. Around that time, a huge green wall rose up to block her way.

Hurry, climb over it!

Following the orders, Sahidi hurried up the large vines in her way, not missing how the guards stopped below as she jumped down the other side. Thinking that she was finally safe now, Sahidi looked around.

There was only gravel and square rocks, overshadowed by the vines growing overhead. And waves. She stopped just before they could lap around her, and the stump of her sixth leg began to ache at the sight. She really hated the ocean.

Suddenly, a noise came from behind her. Now paying close attention to her back eyes, Sahidi observed in shock how the guards passed through the wall of vines like ghosts. It made her remember her mother's warning to not be surprised by new things, but this was just too unexpected, wasn't it?! What was wrong with this place?! Her surprise made Sahidi freeze for a moment, but the harp she still held in her arms readily guided her.

Get into the dinghy! Before they catch you!

Get into what? Sahidi looked forward, spotting something on the shore she somehow hadn't noticed before. As if waiting for her, a small, wooden bowl bobbed in the shallow water, like the thing that carried her here but smaller.

Hurry!

Sahidi flinched but reluctantly followed her brother's advice, wincing through the breaking waves and towards what he had called a dinghy. For some reason, the guards behind her simply watched her leave, like the mindless Rock Puppets they put up at home. Maybe they also were afraid of water?

Refusing to trust that strange idea, Sahidi settled down in the dinghy and lifted its two oars with her small arms. Now, her time at the cave proved useful, and bit by bit, she left the motionless guards behind. Accompanied by the encouraging instructions of her brother, she rowed into the forest of vines, and without him, she would've simply returned to the shore, guards or not.

After many pulls on the oars, the thicket of vines around her finally lightened until the last of them fell away. Sahidi was so drained she simply let the paddles fall down, almost losing them to the sea before she hurriedly pulled them up again. Why did she have to do all of this? She had always been smaller than her sibling to begin with and wasn't even grown yet! Her arms were aching so much she couldn't feel them anymore, not to mention the pain in her legs. How miserable could it get?!

While she was complaining about her fate, a violent sound suddenly ruffled her hair and prompted her to lift her head. Behind the towering vines and above the city, a glowing pillar rose high into the sky, its flames tainted with an eerie violet. Sahidi shuddered as she saw it and realized that, if she hadn't searched for her brother and had continued sleeping, she would still be on that island, so close to that awful gate. All on their own, her aching arms flew back to the rudders, and she began to row despite all her exhaustion. She needed to get away from those violet flames. Before this world ended up just like her old.

THE CONSEQUENCE OF FAILURE

"YOU IDIOT!"

A slap sounded through the tent as another blow hit Yarok's bruised cheek, adding more scratches to his bone-plated face. His remaining armor had been removed as soon as they found him on the ship, and now he was sitting on the floor of the round command tent like a piece of furniture. The commander stood in front of him, her fury still burning as intense as the moment she had started. She was so angry she didn't even care that her hood had come off. As she gave him another slap, her silver-white hair fluttered around like a storm, its color only highlighting the dark, ugly scars that covered every inch of her face. For a while now, she had been beaten him red and blue, but even if his legs had been working, he wouldn't have fled. There simply was no escaping this person.

"YOU HAD! ONE! JOB!" A slap followed each word. "GET THE DEMON, AND LURE OUT THE EDGE! HOW DID YOU MANAGE TO LET RAAKA – THAT BITCH! – ESCAPE IN THE PROCESS?!"

Her voice rose to hysterical levels, but Yarok didn't answer. It would have been useless anyway, for this wasn't the first time the commander asked these questions. This wasn't about answers, just about a way to vent her anger.

"AND THE DAMAGES! REPAIRING THE VINES WILL TAKE WEEKS! ARE YOU AWARE THAT THE EDGIES MERELY NEED TO KNOCK? THAT'S HOW FLIMSY THEY ARE! IT'S SO OBVIOUS, DO YOU THINK THEY WON'T NOTICE?!"

Yarok endured in silence. He had carried out his tasks to the best of his abilities – now, there was only punishment. Another fist hit him, and many more would have followed if not for a shadow that suddenly spoke up from edge of the tent. "Please, honorable Bloodsquare, any more could prove detrimental to our plans." Yarok flinched at the mention of that title, expecting that fool to end up as a corpse real soon. As expected, the commander whipped around in a blur, her ever-stained sword awfully close to the robed man who had spoken.

"I *forbade you* from calling me that way! If you can't remember something that simple, should I carve it into the back of your skull?" But even in the face of this very real threat, the foreigner only chuckled lightly before straightening his robe, apparently without a care in the world. Although the commander could pull it off in theory, the man knew it was an empty threat, and as he laughed, the amulet dangling from his dark hood danced left and right as if to emphasize that fact. The open eye it showed, surrounded by a twisted maze, almost seemed to twinkle in the darkness.

"I will keep it in mind," the foreigner replied eventually when the commander kept her sword trained at his neck. To Yarok, it simply seemed like he had distracted her from her anger, but he wasn't thankful. Less anger did nothing in keeping her from gripping him by his throat, and he heard his useless legs drag over the floor as she easily lifted him closer to her face.

"I warned you, Yarok, didn't I? But you are *obviously* just as senile as our good friend here." The commander pointed at the foreigner with one hand. "But you don't have to worry, my *dear subordinate.* I already know the *perfect* way you can redeem yourself." She didn't sound angry anymore, but her sweet tone made him feel sicker than her anger ever could. "Yes, I am *really* looking forward to it." Seeing her grin, Yarok swallowed dryly. If that bastard had only killed him back then.

Naturally, the commander of the Cursed Coast's alliance was right, and the Vanguard of World's Edge didn't miss the commotion that had revolved around the harbor. The evening of the next day, they were there, an armada of ships that gathered before the gaping breach in the vines. The Edgies didn't even know yet that their biggest obstacle, the Witch who had reaped their lives en masse, was gone as well, or they would have with even bigger numbers.

Staring at the army in front of the shore, the commander was calm. Like a queen, she stood on the longest vine of the harbor, expectantly awaiting the ships approaching in the distance. Her hood had been pulled up again to hide her shameful scars, and only a group of robed foreigners stood behind her, the shade of their gowns like blood in the sunset. Other than them, the harbor was completely deserted. Everyone who wasn't needed had been confined to safety.

With everything prepared to her satisfaction, the commander took her time to appreciate the moment as she stared out at the fleet of the Edge, this one much more imposing than the last. It was so bittersweet and full of irony that it hurt. If she hadn't listened to Raaka, advocate of good, would she still be standing here, so close to get revenge? Although they said that sometimes in life everything fell into place, she had never quite believed it. Almost out of habit, her hand caressed her silvery hair in thought, stroking over the stumps of the limbs that were supposed to grow from her head. Yes, she had never quite believed in fate. Up to this day.

"We are ready at your signal," the leader of the foreigners spoke up, the one who had also been present when the commander had 'talked' to Yarok.

But her gaze remained straight as an arrow even when he stopped right next to her.

"Let them come closer," she replied curtly. After she had waited so long, how stupid would it be to risk it all just because of a few minutes of her time. This moment was the beginning of her crusade, and she had to savor every last drop of it. Much too soon for her liking, the ships of the Edge were there, so close she could even hear the voices of the soldiers on board. The thought of ending them for good finally brought a smile to her scarred face. "It's time to take out the trash," she uttered happily. "Do what you came here for."

"Very well," the robed man answered with a bow, causing the people standing behind him to explode into six of pillars of flame that unified in the sky. Hearing the screams of his subordinates, their leader turned around, lifting his arms to the focal point above as the jagged runes smeared on the vines flashed with a crimson light. "Oh we who evade the Gates of the Den! Our fading souls call out to Gavrog, Lord of All Mayhem! This table, our table, has been set!"

Let the Harvest begin!

Hey there.

This is the author speaking. If you read this, then you have made me very happy – for you likely read all the way till here.
There is, however, a problem: I don't even know if you liked or hated it – and personally, I tend to expect the latter.

Am I wrong? Then, please leave a review on Amazon, consider writing on Discord or by email, or even leave a little support on Patreon. You just have to scan the code below with your mobile phone camera, and give some constructive feedback. It is always much appreciated.

I pray that we may read again
-L.B.

Printed in Great Britain
by Amazon